CAN I
SEE THE
WOOD
FOR THE
TREES

Best wishes

R. Taylor

carpe Diem

Published in paperback in 2023 by Sixth Element Publishing
on behalf of R. T. Taylor

Sixth Element Publishing
Arthur Robinson House
13-14 The Green
Billingham TS23 1EU
www.6epublishing.net

ISBN 978-1-914170-50-8

British Library Cataloguing in Publication Data. A catalogue record for
this book is available from the British Library.

Printed in Great Britain.

CAN'T
SEE THE
WOOD
FOR THE
TREES

R.T. TAYLOR

This book is dedicated to the memory of my mother, Rosalyn.
I love and miss you every day.

And to my two boys, Connor and Charlie.
You can achieve anything.
Do what makes you happy.

INTRODUCTION BY VICTORIA COLLIN

Hartlepool is a small town. It's impossible to live your whole life there and not find a familiar face wherever you go but the writer's group was a completely unconventional space I'd never used before and it was fantastic!

Rob was a new face among many. We were all a big mix of people. I say a big mix – we were all working class white people from the town and interested in writing. The most differing thing between us all was age and writing style. This was pre-pandemic when we could socialise in the town library, and that's where we met.

I was tutoring English at the time when Rob asked for a business card and fresh eyes to read over his manuscript, and I nearly bit his hand off when he asked. In terms of careers, the only real prospect to make a living at anything literary based is teaching English in mainstream classrooms – at least where we are. Anyway, I gave him my card and time flew.

I read his e-mail a few months later in my junk inbox and thought 'CRAP! I need to e-mail him back'. It wasn't long before we video-called to discuss what exactly it was that he was looking for. So my role, I think, has evolved from a creative one-to-one tutor to coffee buddy – when we'd have our sessions in Starbucks – to developmental editor, and the pandemic had a large role to play in that change. Instead of meeting in person, our working interactions

were notes on pages (mostly me writing 'GET RID!!!' on purple highlighted sticky notes) and monthly video call meetings. This was a huge learning curve for us both because he'd never had his work edited in a thorough one-to-one style before, nor had I edited anything like it on this scale.

The first draft I saw was a printed manuscript in a green paper folder and it couldn't have been more than twenty-five pages long. No chapters, no sectioning, just a very rough draft of a bloody great story! Inclusion, tragedy, loss, small town problems… I was hooked and after the first read, it was a story I knew I was emotionally invested in.

Rob had said that he was starting the writer's race late and it was this very rough draft in my hands that had been playing on his mind for a good portion of his adult life. Looking at the hours we have both put into it – after all the extensions, the rewrites, the discussions of where the story is going next and picking away at all the possibilities – it really is amazing to see what his vision, as fantastical and almost cinematic as it is, has achieved.

CHAPTER 1

Lying on the bed of his converted cupboard bedroom, Joseph stares up at the ceiling and holds the carved wooden animals up into the air, making them move and using pretend voices like they're talking to each other.

"Joseph," shouts his mum, Daisy. "Joseph Adams! For the love of Queen Vic, get up now or you will be late for school."

"Right!" he shouts, followed by a heavy sigh; school is the one place he hates because of the relentless bullying and teasing. Kicking his blankets off, he places the figures onto the narrow windowsill under the eaves of the thatched roof of the old English cottage. He received them as recompense from William, the carpenter, in exchange for his weekends spent in the workshop. Joseph climbs out of his bed and onto the high wooden roof trusses which had been fashioned into a ladder of metal rods. Dressed and washed, he heads downstairs for breakfast.

Navigating his way past his brothers' and sisters' bedrooms, his eyes focus straight ahead, and he holds his head firmly high. The dreaded morning walk down the hall always feels like passing a pack of wild wolves. They shout the usual teasing and hurtful remarks as they carry out their morning routines, usually consisting of rowdy squabbling and shouting, complaints to their parents about each other and then pushing one another out of the way. 'Mother says I should just ignore them and that it's just family being family. At least they're not as bad as the others at school,' Joseph thinks to himself.

Once in the kitchen, he finds his mum pottering around the room, giving the porridge, which is cooking on the stove, a stir as she passes by it.

Hearing Joseph come in, she turns around to make eye contact and says, "Good morning, love. The porridge is ready."

He eases into a chair wearing a grin as he observes his mum moving around the kitchen. His mum is a slim lady with a tapered waist, her figure shown to full effect in her favourite full length dark blue dress. She has a soft and warm face that lights up the room and a smile that can make anybody feel good. Her long brown hair is tied up in a bun, with loose strands waving in the air unable to stay fastened down. She is always sweet and kind to Joseph and always brings out the best in him.

"Your father has left for work already, so you'll have to serve your own porridge," she adds.

His father, Richard, is an assistant to the blacksmith, Arthur. Richard is a tall, thin man with soot blackened skin, his rugged face showing the signs of wear due to the long hours and hard work. He always tries to dress smartly but always comes home filthy black and stinking of burnt coal and sweat from the forge he works at. His hands are rough and well worn. He is often up and out early (to go to work if Arthur has lots of work on). Joseph helped out at the forge once but burnt his hand, and that was enough to scare him away for good. Now, he'll only brave the forge with his mother on the occasional weekend, and even then he would still hold a nervous breath every time on passing the threshold.

"Great. I'm starving," replies Joseph with a smile on his face as he fetches a bowl and spoon.

His two brothers and three sisters come barging in, pushing and shoving with elbows while chatting and squabbling, turning the kitchen into a cattle market. With the sound of all the commotion, Joseph peeks in their direction. He is pushed and shoved out of the way and receives a barrage of insults and nasty comments from his siblings.

"Come on, move out of the way, boy!"

"Move, maggot!"

"Oh! Get out of my way."

Joseph is left holding his bowl and spoon.

"Leave him be," snaps his mother, jumping to her youngest son's defence.

They gather and sit around the table to tuck into their porridge. Joseph helps himself to the lumpy leftovers and perches on the small stool in the corner. Having survived yet another breakfast routine at home, he heads off to school following his siblings.

The walk to school always feels like the wrath of God dragging him to meet his maker. Walking down the main street of his small old English town, Hopewood, he gazes at the thatched houses and shops filling the dirt lined street: shoemakers, milliners, haberdashers, bakers, butchers, grocers, booksellers with the odd horse and cart outside and other streets branching off. They saunter past the main square which has a statue of a smart bearded soldier, with a hat and holding a sword, sitting astride a rampant bronze horse, in honour of the first mayor of Hopewood, General Robin Williams.

The school is situated just beyond the main square, on the main street. A large white walled converted barn, it has half a dozen rooms made into classrooms spread over two floors. On arrival, Joseph thinks to himself, doubtful while taking a deep breath, 'I really do hope class will be better.'

All the children pack into the small schoolroom upstairs in the barn, and, while waiting for the teacher, most of them turn their attention to Joseph, teasing him and pulling his clothes, with a few insults thrown in for good measure.

The teacher, Miss Muggleton, enters the room. She is a smartly attired woman in a flowing floral dress, perfectly fitted. Her hair is always tied neatly at the back without a strand out of place, although, she always seems to have a scowl on her face. Then, as if the children are attached to elastic, they quickly return to their seats and desks. Joseph sits quietly next to a window and glances momentarily to the outside, falling into a daydream about jousting knights while Miss Muggleton talks to the class. She suddenly throws a book in Joseph's direction! He instinctively sits up and, with a shock, his eyebrows jump, his eyes fly open, his jaw clenches and his face blushes bright red with embarrassment.

"Do I have your attention now?" she asks.

He nods quickly, unable to speak through the dryness weighing on his tongue.

"Good morning, class," Miss Muggleton announces.

"Good morning, Miss Muggleton," they all reply.

•

On his way home, enjoying the spring sunshine, he ponders why every day is so difficult. The relentless dread and constant bullying haunting his dreams cause dark shadows under his eyes. His head is downcast as he walks alone, passing William's carpentry workshop. William is a tall, broad, muscular man with a rugged stubbly beard making him seem aged beyond his years. In spite of his height and stature, and a complexion like wrinkled coffee-stained paper, there is a warmth in his everyday demeanour. Often presentable and tidy, a cowlick escapes the muddy mop of hair that is brushed back neatly. Dressed in a collarless shirt and heavy cotton trousers with his usual carpenter's apron over the top, he is standing in the doorway, enjoying a break with a glass of water in the afternoon sunshine. Encouraging eye contact, William can sense Joseph's suffering (as he does most days) and grins in his direction.

"Afternoon, Joseph. How are you?"

"I'm all right." His brave smile temporarily draws

William's attention away from his dark sunken eyes which glaze over the second the smells of different types of wood drowns his senses, admiringly in awe of the different grain patterns. He is fascinated by how many things are made from wood and enjoys the feeling of the smoothness as it glides through his hands... 'but not to take it for granted or it'll give you splinters and then William has to take them out.'

Joseph slows his walk to ponder at the workshop, shifts his weight from side to side and glances sheepishly at William.

"Come in if you want? I could do with a hand if you have a few minutes?" smiles William.

"Yes, no problem," beams Joseph. His face lights up! The interior is serene. No bullies. No savage siblings.

He sighs deeply, gravitating towards the different tables and workbenches and racks of different sized chisels, and hammers and mallets with an array of sizes and wood planers on the walls and a collection of saws that have to be seen to be believed.

William guides him over to a set of lopsided drawers and asks Joseph to hold the drawers steadily before hammering the wooden joints together, using a mallet and a scrap lump of wood as a cushion.

"I called up to see your mother today. I told her how happy I am with the help you have given me over the past few weeks," says William.

Receiving such a compliment felt so rare, Joseph couldn't help but beam with pride.

"I've asked them if you could help me gather materials from the Wood for a job I'm working on… and they said they're happy to let you work with me for the day, if it's something you'd like to do?"

"Really?" answers Joseph. His eyes widen with excitement and wonder at the thought of learning something new with William, his best friend.

"Can you meet me here first thing Saturday morning at about seven, please?" asks William.

"Yes, all right. Thank you," says Joseph.

On his way home, Joseph can't help but smile to himself. It's been a long time since he had felt this happy, feeling so needed, feeling a sense of responsibility. All the way home Joseph would catch the eye of the different townsfolk who would notice his grin and glint in his eye and they couldn't help but to return a little grin which fuelled Joseph's happiness even more. Even at home, dealing with the mayhem couldn't shatter his smile, nor could the rowdiness at bedtime as he fell soundly asleep.

The following Saturday morning arrives when the cock-a-doodle-doo of a cockerel rouses a light sleeping Joseph. Quickly jumping out of bed, he throws on some old well-worn clothes. The house, seemingly to Joseph, has a new strangeness in the quiet early hours, perhaps strange in the absence of his worrying or the usual challenges. As the feral creatures that are his relatives lay snoring in their beds, he slips downstairs to find his mother in the kitchen.

"Morning, Mum," says Joseph, still wearing the same smile.

"You're up early! Would you like some breakfast?" says his Mum.

"No thanks," he says grabbing an apple from the bowl on the side. "This is my breakfast today," he says with the same big grin as yesterday. "I'm maybe too early, but I really don't want to be late," he continues with a sense of purpose in his voice.

"Go and enjoy your day and learn all you can," advises his Mum. Beaming with pride, she gives Joseph a big hug. Without another word, they smile at each other and Joseph leaves to meet William.

Arriving at the workshop, Joseph, in his old rugged dungarees, sees William.

"Ah, you're here! Nice and early, too," says William.

Joseph grins with a glint of anticipation in his eyes.

"Well, if you're ready, let's get going!" Together they push a four-wheeled cart that is loaded with a bag of strong rope and wooden wedges (to help with splitting the wood) and a long saw, and they set off along the street towards the Wood.

Joseph tries to contain his excitement by tuning his ears to hear the morning birds' song. Making idle small talk, they make their way to the Wood, which fringes the outskirts of the town. They gradually approach a line of thickly barked trees with the odd broken branch pointing down towards the dense vegetation and bushes that cover the Wood's base like a heavy green carpet. There is a light breeze swaying the trees back and forth, making a blustery rustling sound. Although Joseph has been lots of times before, this time feels different.

Leaving the cart on the beaten track they take the tool bag and large saw and make their way through the Wood. Within a few yards, it is noticeably darker and they have to be careful of their footing. Joseph listens in anticipation for the softness of the forest bed, waiting for the muffled snap it sometimes makes as he ventures forward. They help each other over each obstacle and sometimes hold on to one another for support, stepping gingerly over old logs and branches while William points out different species of tree.

"They're mainly poplar trees in the Wood – ideal to make a log house with. Bet you could build one yourself by now," he jokes.

As they tread deeper into the Wood, William points out more interesting things they find and notice.

"Look over there, Joseph," he says, pointing towards a thick wide tree. "That's an oak tree. Oak is harder than elm, but elm has an interlocking grain that makes it much, much tougher than oak. But today we're looking for a beech tree to make a cabinet. There's one not too far from here and it's already down so we'll cut it up and take it back with us."

Feeling quite out of his depth, Joseph just nods and smiles at William's every word, absorbing as much wisdom as he can.

William, a few paces ahead, leads the way through the

Wood as Joseph swings a branch side to side to clear his own path. A few minutes pass before William notices Joseph pulling away at the spare leaves and off shooting twigs from his weapon of choice.

Joseph's breathing becomes more laboured from each swing... his daydreaming mind starts to wander: the stick transforms into an elaborately gilded sword and he imagines himself as a gallant soldier. Each bush, each overhanging branch is vanquished with a heroic stab to the heart, amputating limb after thorny limb.

"Take that! And that, you maggot!"

Meanwhile, William smiles a little to himself. Joseph, lost in his own world, absentmindedly veers away from William to slay the enemy shrubs off the beaten track. Joseph is shocked as his daydream comes to a sudden stop. His opponents are neither dead nor alive – just green. The light is sparse. He is just Joseph.

"W...W... Will...?"

"JOSEPH!" William jumps from behind a tree, brandishing a much larger, more intimidating stick with a face like thunder, brows murderous and a vein ready to explode under his cowlick.

"ARGHHH!" Joseph ditches his humble blade and hides under a leafy carcass.

William slowly steps towards the quivering boy hiding in the vegetation.

"Draw. Your. Sword."

Joseph looks at William, expecting to be scolded, only to be met with William standing in a fencing stance.

"EN GARDE!" William pokes his backside with the pointy end of his stick.

A gleeful look appears on Joseph's face as he realises William's innocent intention to spar.

The pair jostle around, swinging their weapons to block and strike each other. Being the more experienced of the pair, William is agile and quick to whack his little friend in the stomach, in the armpit, under the chin, and he expertly feigns deep seething pain when Joseph returns the gesture. Stepping back slightly, William trips over a log hidden under moss. Seizing the opportunity, Joseph climbs onto the stump of a tree and springs up into the air, simultaneously swinging his sword over his head as if to mark a final battle blow. Joseph lands on both feet next to William and points his sword towards his throat.

"Do you yield?" shouts Joseph to a surprised-looking William who bursts into laughter.

He climbs to his feet with a little help from Joseph, patting down his clothes to brush off the clinging shrubbery and leaves.

William giggles and throws his arm around Joseph's shoulders, saying "Let's go and find this tree." They both wade through the Wood, waving and swinging their swords merrily as they go.

CHAPTER 2

They find the felled tree, saw it into pieces and lug it back to the cart. They take a moment to rest and gather their thoughts. William takes some water from his satchel and offers Joseph a drink.

Joseph happily receives it and pauses for a moment looking down at the ground. Turning to his friend, he looks at William with a grateful wide smile and says, "Thank you for today! I've really enjoyed it," before taking a drink of the water.

"You're welcome," replies William, who clenches his lips, understanding the sincerity of Joseph's voice.

Joseph is grinning from ear to ear as the memories of their little adventure race through his head.

"Don't thank me just yet," William exclaims. "We still have to get this lot back to my workshop." He has another quick drink and places it back in the satchel.

Together, they push the heavy cart laden with the logs towards town. They finally approach the workshop and retrieve the lumps of wood and pile them neatly in the inside corner. They both stand upright and lean back slightly to stretch their backs from the heavy lifting. William looks over to Joseph, impressed by his hard work and willingness to help.

"Joseph, can you pull in the cart, please?" asks William.

"Yes, no problem," replies Joseph as he heads for the large doorway. He pulls the cart in slowly but surely and parks it at the side of the workshop. He turns to find William over on the other side of the workshop holding a box covered by a hessian cloth.

"Come over here, Joseph," says William. As Joseph approaches him, he continues, "I'd like to show you this box I've just finished." He takes the cover off, revealing a beautifully polished box with an inlaid scene of different trees, a minuscule depiction of General Williams' rampant horse in the centre, with the word 'Hopewood' embellished at the bottom.

"It's a truly beautiful box, William," says Joseph with a look of real amazement, hypnotised by the detail. Joseph touches the smooth polished surface gently.

"It's yours," states William.

Joseph fills up with so much emotion that his eyes well up.

"Really? Why?" Joseph stutters.

For all your hard work. It's to keep all those figures in that I made for you," says William.

Joseph throws his arms around William and gives him the biggest hug he can muster, almost knocking the box out of his hand. So low it is barely an audible whisper, he says to himself, "The greatest day ever." They both make their way out of the workshop, Joseph tucking the hessian wrapped box tightly under his arm.

"Joseph! Joseph!" comes the gentle shout of his mother

from the other side of the street. After greeting them, she thanks William for giving Joseph such a memorable morning.

Joseph interrupts, "Look what William has made for me!"

As he unwraps the beautiful box with shaking hands full of excitement, she gasps.

"That's really beautiful." She looks at Joseph and William with proud eyes, then says, "Now, help me with this basket…"

Following an unforgettable weekend, the everyday horrors of school return again on the following Monday. Over the coming days and weeks, every time something happens, he uses that weekend full of memories to feel better. The box with his carved figures inside sits in pride of place on top of the chest of drawers in the cupboard that is his room. As the weeks turn into months, the daily bullying takes its toll. The one thing Joseph lives through his bad days for is visiting the workshop. The more frequent Joseph's visits become, the more William notices a change in the boy's demeanour: a longing sigh, his fingers picked raw and bloody, jumping out of his skin at sudden loud noises like a deer.

One day, on his way home from school, a couple of boys are making fun of him. When he doesn't respond, they push him while some of the other children laugh. Joseph looks over at the workshop but it's locked up. He ducks his head down and tries to hurry on without making himself conspicuous. They push him time and time again, just when one of the boys sneakily drops to all fours behind Joseph. One last shove of the shoulder and Joseph is tumbling backwards. Over the eruption of manic laughter, he picks himself up, dusts himself down and shouts, "Leave me alone!"

In a blink, he is surrounded by all the boys and girls, who are egging each other on. The pushing turns into hitting, and laughs are joined by shouting.

"Get him!"

"Hit him!"

"Make him bleed."

Falling to the floor, Joseph curls into a ball and gives a whimpering groan after each hit.

"Hey!" A distant shout makes them all scatter.

Overwhelmed, beaten and worn down, Joseph falls into unconsciousness.

Opening his eyes, he focuses on the light of the moon shining in through the window. He is back in his bedroom and in his bed; it's the middle of the night. His legs and arms ache with pain. Choking on the terrified lump in his throat, a tear rolls down his cheek. And his bottom lip starts to quiver. Unable to swallow his feelings, he sobs. Different thoughts run through his mind: his brothers and sisters squabbling, William under a mist of sawdust, the hissing faces of his tormentors. Slowly, the tears stop and a well of anger froths up from his gut and fizzes into his brain like a vengeful volcano. A storm of thoughts brews a tempest in his mind. The more the thoughts spin around, the more he starts to think of revenge; revenge or carry on as normal and try to forget about it all? The thoughts roll over and over and over in his mind.

'I'd like to get my own back on everyone… I could start with my brothers and sisters. I could tie their shoelaces together, it would be so funny to see them all fall over'. He imagines them all falling like dominoes. 'It might even be worth getting into trouble with mother and father for it. If the other children attack me again, I could run into the Wood – the bestest place in the world! I'd find a good solid stick and use the Wood for my very own version of hide and seek.'

Joseph imagines himself hiding behind different trees, using the dense undergrowth to avoid being seen and jumping out to scare and hit them.

'I'd hurt their arms, their legs and their bodies and let them feel all the pain they gave to me. I want to hurt them like they hurt me.' Joseph clenches his fists for a few seconds as his emotions swell. 'But if I hit them – if I hurt them – then I'm the bad one. The Bible says so. The Bible says that God punishes the wicked. They are wicked. God should punish them. Or maybe… maybe God has sent them to punish me. Maybe I *am* wicked? Maybe this is my punishment. Do mother and father know? Maybe having a wicked son makes them sad. I know being a monster makes me sad. But… I can't just forget that I'm not one. Revenge or forget about it? Revenge? Or forget? If I can't hurt anyone and I can't forget about it all… then the only thing I can do is run away. If I go, I would never see mother and father, and they both help me. My mother is kind and my father is funny… I suppose I would be helping them.'

Then his eyes widen when he realises he would have to leave behind William. 'He's my best friend. He teaches me things and allows me to be myself and to make mistakes and he doesn't ever shout at me – not once. He's very kind and patient.' Suddenly, his attention is grabbed by the wind whirling up debris at his window. Along with the feelings of humiliation, anger and frustration, he takes it as a sign. He slips out of bed quietly, then quickly packs a few clothes into a bag and climbs up to the window to make his escape. As he opens the window, leans out and looks down, he thinks with a gulp, 'That looks a bit high,' so he turns around and creeps downstairs, out the front door and disappears into the night.

The next morning, Joseph's mother is preparing breakfast and she gives her usual morning routine shout, "Joseph, if you don't get up now, you'll be late for school!"

As she works and potters around the kitchen, she realises she hasn't heard any of the usual noises of Joseph getting out of bed. No heavy feet or movement at all – only the rowdy sounds from the other children. She no sooner shouts again when there's a miniature stampede of legs and bodies as the others descend on the kitchen for their breakfasts. In amongst all the commotion of the breakfast routine, Daisy's motherly instinct stirs but since she is busy dealing with the stove, breakfast, and chores, she asks Frederick (the eldest) to go and check on Joseph. With a grunt and a groan, he makes his way up to Joseph's bedroom. He throws open Joseph's bedroom door and takes a deep breath ready to hurl a resentful comment about having to check in on him. But that turns into a quick exhale of shock and surprise at finding the room completely empty.

There is a faint chill to the air, the window has a light rattle to it from the heavier gusts of wind, the bed is made up and the room is tidy.

"Mother?" Frederick shouts, before running back downstairs.

She no sooner shouts back, "What is it?"

When Frederick is back in the kitchen, everyone stares at his blank face.

"He's not there!" he says.

His mother looks confused, trying to think… a million questions running through her head.

"The room is cold because he's left the window open. He's probably gone to see William for some sympathy and attention," he adds.

Daisy knows that something is not right. She refocuses her gaze onto Frederick and says to him urgently, "Go and fetch your father from the blacksmiths. Be quick about it, for Heaven's sake!"

Daisy, in a state of shock, heads along to William's workshop. When she arrives, she is faced with the big, beautifully carved, wooden entrance doors and can hear the sounds of someone sawing wood. She starts to rub her thumb in the centre of her palm and tucks a loose lock of hair behind her ear. Then, taking a deep breath to calm herself, she uses her shoulder to push the large heavy door open, and steps inside.

Noticing the sudden flood of daylight, William turns and looks directly into Daisy's eyes. She takes a second to coyly tidy her hair again and glances down at the ground, pressing her cool palms to her cheek. However, she sighs deeply and clears her throat to speak. "Have you seen Joseph today? He wasn't in his room this morning and I'm worried sick."

William shakes his head, frowning. "No. Sorry," he says, removing his apron.

"I don't want to impose on you. But please, I know what he's like around you. He listens to you more than he listens to me most of the time," Daisy replies.

William nods as he walks over to Daisy and, sensing her distress, he calmly hugs her and says, "He's a clever lad, you know. He'll be right as rain."

She can't help but return the hug, resting her head on his chest and eases into his embrace.

Catching herself, she pulls away abruptly and says, "I need to go and find him."

William nods and placing his hand on her lower back, he ushers her out of the door.

They knock on doors and feel a sense of uneasiness as the people shy away from their twitching curtains, cowering from the persistent knocks or feigning feeble excuses for their unhelpfulness. Eventually, with some determination, they gather eight people – mainly William's friends – to meet Richard in the main square. Street after street, they begin the search for Joseph. At around lunchtime, they meet back in the town square.

Richard says, "We should start looking in the Wood," while Daisy simply weeps in his arms. They all agree, retreat to gather different tools, returning with hoes and hand scythes. William passes a hand scythe and a long stick to Richard.

Richard turns to Daisy to say, "You should go home in case he returns."

With a kiss, she heads home while the others head for the Wood. They return home as the afternoon light fades – without Joseph.

The next day, the same eight people meet outside the Adams' house and stride past the gossip and whispers back toward the Wood. When they return (again, without success) they notice even more people out, huddled in small groups of three and four people. Some of them make pointed side glances as they chat amongst themselves. Some of them make loud declarations for the returning men to overhear.

"Good riddance – whole lot of them are bad rubbish, I say."

"If he's left, he has done us all a favour. Let's pray to God he's jumped in a river."

"It be the mother's fault. I'd say she's a witch."

"He was unnatural – 'tis the work of the devil, that boy."

"Someone ought to burn them all at the stake."

The atmosphere around the town continues to escalate for days. Daisy battles sleepless nights, tormented with anxiety, met with unease from the other townsfolk she once considered her friends. Feeling she has no other choice, she withdraws as much as she possibly can, only leaving home when absolutely necessary. The children stop attending school due to the backlash, the town's children bullying and taunting them, and even some getting into fights on a more frequent basis. After a week, Richard loses his job when Arthur cracks under the pressure, having received angry anonymous letters about him. Some include threats to his business from the community and demand he disassociate himself from 'the devil worshipping' family.

Finally, one evening, everything builds into a raucous climax. As the group of men return from the search, the air of the town seems eerily quiet. They make their way through the town and the men break off from the group to return to their homes until only Richard and William are left outside in the open. The two of them continue along the street, past the town square, when Richard notices an angry crowd of maybe two dozen people outside his home, all standing around with rope, pitchforks and hand scythes… some are even carrying flaming torches. Each person has a copy of the Bible under their arms for spiritual protection. Richard's heart sinks like a stone. His first thought is for his terrified family. He hurries as fast as his tired and hurting legs will carry him. Approaching them, the angry mob turn to his direction, some of them waving their copy of the Bible. Stopping in his tracks, taken aback, he abandons his plan to reach his front door.

"What's going on here?" Richard bravely confronts them.

Some of the men at the flank of the mob point the pitchforks at William and Richard. Without saying a word, William takes a small step back.

"You and your family and that witch in there," shouts a man, obviously the leader, who William recognises as Mr Miller.

Richard looks at the angry mob through tears in his eyes, then at his home with his terrified family peeking from the corners of the windows, trying not to be seen.

"What do you want from us?" he reluctantly asks.

"Either we try her for being a witch," Miller says, as one or two of the others point their pitchforks and torches at the house, "for birthing a monster from the devil and allowing it to escape to God only knows where…" Miller holds up a bible and spits, "Or!"

He pauses for a moment…

"Or what!" asks Richard aggressively.

Miller looks around the group for nods of confirmation.

"Or you *all* leave Hopewood. Tonight!" he demands. Then the group part to reveal a beaten and damaged cart with an old and weary horse at the front.

Richard realises he doesn't have any option and, wanting to protect his family, he reluctantly says, "We'll leave tonight."

The angry men lower their weapons only slightly as Richard makes his way past them and enters his house.

Once through the door, his children gather around him with fearful looks on their faces, closely followed by their mother.

"We have to leave, tonight," Richard announces sternly but calmly.

Frantic, yet stone faced, Daisy holds a whimpering child, and spits out, "We can't leave… I can't just leave. Where will we go? What about Joseph?"

"We have no choice," Richard replies.

"Well, you take the children and I can stay behind to wait for Joseph," she says defiantly.

"I don't think that's a good idea, it's not safe," he murmurs to her under his breath. "We can send word to William about Joseph, but right now your other children need you just as much as Joseph does. You are no good to anyone dead." Richard takes hold of her hands gently and reassuringly continues, "It'll be alright. As long as we're together, we have all we'll ever need."

Daisy packs what she can into a couple of cases while the angry mob become more restless outside.

As they leave, the men move to one side to let the family onto the cart with their battered cases.

William hurries to the front of the cart where Daisy is sitting and says with a whisper to both of them, "I'm so sorry. I can't believe this is what it is all coming to," and shakes Richard's hand firmly. They share a look of concealed mutual understanding. "Good luck!" William adds.

William clasps his hands onto Daisy's, and is surprised to feel a folded piece of paper in her left palm.

Daisy sobs uncontrollably as she lets go, finger by finger, of William, the folded paper and Hopewood, .

Richard replies, "If he comes back, please make sure he's taken care of and not given up to this lot."

William nods, and whispers, "Send me word when you get to your destination."

Richard climbs up and with a crack of the reins, they slowly disappear into the night.

As their silhouettes fade into the darkness, never to be seen or heard from again, William looks down at the folded letter in his hand.

CHAPTER 3

Fifteen years later

It's a bright sunny morning. The children line up outside the school and wait to be called in. Miss Muggleton steps out, immaculately presented and wearing a beautiful conservative dress, and she rings a large bell to signal the start of the school day.

Once in class, they all find their seats and wait for the teacher while chattering amongst themselves about the new girl in the room. Miss Muggleton walks in confidently and sits in her chair behind a desk. She takes a moment to look around, waiting for everyone to be quiet, having gained a calmer demeanour over the years. She then stands and says, "Good morning, class."

The children jump to their feet and reply, "Good morning, Miss Muggleton." Some try to peek at the new girl.

Miss Muggleton then goes through the register, calling out each child in turn alphabetically. "Finally, we have Zelda Williams," she announces.

The new girl stands promptly and replies, "Here, Miss." Zelda no sooner sits in her seat when out of the corner of her eye, she spots workmen outside unloading sacks of flour for the bakers. She continues to gawk at the men, who seem to have perfected a system. Each one grabs a sack, pulls it onto his shoulders using both hands to lean forward and disappears through the doorway, the process repeated by the next man. She drifts into a daydream and imagines the men as busy bees who scurry around, and an imaginary queen bee standing nearby as she organises them, prodding them with a stick.

"Before we start, I have an announcement and a big surprise for you all! For those of you who didn't know, we have a new family move into town all the way from Hartlepool… this is Zelda Williams. Now, Zelda is a very special girl… her ancestry dates back to the first Mayor of Hopewood! Would you believe it? In my class," says Miss Muggleton, smiling proudly, glancing up at the heavens while placing her hand on her chest. "Why don't you stand up to introduce yourself and perhaps tell us something about yourself?" she adds.

Silence quickly fills the room as Zelda is still looking out of the window.

"Zelda!" Miss Muggleton announces with a slightly raised voice.

Still, no response. Everyone starts to look in Zelda's direction.

"Zelda," sings Miss Muggleton loudly while slapping a wooden ruler on her desk to grab Zelda's attention.

As Zelda turns to face the teacher, Miss Muggleton is touching her cheek and immaculate hair with the palm of her hand to help calm her embarrassment.

"Would you like to tell the class something about yourself?" she says, regaining her composure.

"Hello, everyone. My name is Zelda Williams and I love nature and animals. I also really enjoy climbing trees and helping my father with his hobby, taxidermy," says Zelda, a quick-witted, confident and intelligent young girl with a shock of vibrant red hair, and neatly presented in a full length royal blue dress with slight scratches on her arms.

"Thank you, Zelda," says Miss Muggleton continuing to proudly smile. "I'm sure the other children will help you settle in," she adds.

At lunchtime, Zelda bumps into Fiona.

"Sorry!" they both say at the same time, which brings a smile to each of their faces.

"Hi, I'm Zelda," she says quickly with a smile, hoping to make her first friend.

"I'm Fiona. My lord, I've never seen someone with red hair before! So pretty!" she replies while flicking her hair over her ear and moves her face to the side slightly, too shy to hold eye contact.

"Nice dress! It's just like mine but I love it better in navy," says Zelda, as she reaches for Fiona's dress and caresses the beautiful fabric between her fingers.

Fiona glances to make eye contact and replies, "Thanks." Fiona then looks around the room to find her group of friends.

She turns and asks Zelda, "Would you like to come and join us?"

Seizing the opportunity to make more friends, Zelda replies, "That would be great, thanks."

They join a small group of children, who are sitting at the end of a long table lined with benches, and start to make small talk since the others are in full conversation.

Spencer, who is sitting at the end of the table like the group leader, tilting his chair back onto two legs, throws his voice over the group's volume, "Who's your new friend, Fiona?"

Fiona withdraws into her shy self but Zelda is quick to help and replies for her.

"I'm Zelda," she says with confidence. "And you are?"

"Um… Spencer. I'm Spencer," he responds while sitting upright. He then continues to introduce everyone else in the group. "Fiona, you've met."

They look at each other with a grin.

"This is Victoria – but don't mind what she says. She always speaks her mind but she never means to be nasty. This is Thomas, and this is Lisa."

They all say 'hello' after they've been introduced. Spencer resumes the conversation, including Fiona and Zelda. "We are going to the Wood at the weekend. Are you both coming?" he asks.

Fiona nods in agreement but Zelda says, "I will have to ask my parents but I can't see why not."

"What do your mother and father do?" asks Spencer.

"My mother is called Esme. She looks after the home and myself. And my father is called Robert – he's a Doctor," Zelda explains.

"Where did you move from again?" asks Victoria.

"Hartlepool. It's a small town in the northeast of

England. We moved here for my father's work. He's travelled the world! He could work anywhere he wanted. Strange places called Timbuktu and Prussia... But my Mum hates sailing, hence we moved here," Zelda explains. Then, looking away, she giggles to herself.

Spencer notices her giggling and, thinking she is making a fool out of them, says accusingly, "What's so funny?"

"Did you know... that the people of Hartlepool are called 'monkey hangers'?" giggles Zelda.

The others look at each other and laugh.

"Be off with you," says Lisa.

"You're having us on," Thomas says.

"Yeah, right!" says Spencer.

Just then, Miss Muggleton strolls out and rings the bell for everyone to return to class.

After school, the children quickly disperse in the direction of their homes. Having found out that Fiona lives a little further along Hawkes Lane from Zelda, the two decide to walk home together. Approaching Zelda's house, she asks Fiona, "Would you like to come and meet my parents quickly?"

Fiona replies with a shy smile, "Yes please."

Fiona follows Zelda into her home and they're immediately hit with the sweet smell of freshly baked cake. As they follow the sweet smell coming from the kitchen, Fiona notices a black and white picture on the wall. It is a group of men and women smartly dressed, with the words 'Missionaries of Timbuktu' underneath.

As they walk into the kitchen, they find Mrs Williams placing a freshly baked lemon cake onto a plate. Fiona's eyes are wide open with amazement. Smells of sugar and citrus engulfs the room.

"Would you girls like some lemon cake?" she asks.

They both answer together, "Yes please."

They sit at the kitchen table (which half fills the room) and together they eat the still-warm-from-the-oven lemon cake. Esme then starts to potter around the kitchen, doing some general chores.

Fiona asks, "What's the picture in the passageway about?"

"My father was in the missionaries to help people in different countries – some of them were quite poor. He's travelled all over the world: America, Africa, Europe and the far East. He then worked onboard a ship to get back to England but it only docked in at Hartlepool. He got off there and soon met my mother. It was always my father's plan to settle here because we have the family connection, here, and more family in a nearby town so he became a local doctor."

Fiona's eyes light with pure awe. "Wow, that's amazing! Thank you for the cake, Mrs Williams, it was delicious. I must go home, now. My parents will be wondering where I am. I'll see you tomorrow at school, Zelda."

Fiona is no sooner out the door when Esme asks, "How was school?"

"It's fine. The other kids seem friendly, too, but they have asked me to go with them to the Wood at the weekend. May I?" She adds.

"No. Your father and I have heard some disturbing stories and what not about that place and I don't want you going there, yes?" says Esme.

"Oh, it'll be alright! There will be six of us going and we can look after each other," says Zelda.

"I said no. It is not safe and, as I have said already, I've heard stories," says Esme in a stern tone.

"But that's all they are – *stories*!" says Zelda.

"The answer is no," snaps Esme firmly.

With that, Zelda storms off to her room.

The next day is bright and sunny and, at school during lunch, the five of them are chatting with each other when Lisa suggests, "Why don't we meet up after school on the small common on the edge of town at about six o'clock?"

They all agree that it's a great idea.

Later that day, Zelda asks her mother: "May I please go down to the common later?"

"Yes, but you aren't to go in the Wood," says Esme.

"Yes, I know," replies Zelda.

When there is a knock on the door, Zelda opens it to see Fiona and they both walk down to the common to see that everyone is already there, laughing and larking around. They all sit and throw all the snack foods together in the centre of their circle.

Zelda places some of her mother's lemon cake down which prompts Fiona to say, "Everyone needs to try Zelda's mother's cake – it's delicious!"

They all start chatting amongst themselves when Victoria interjects in Zelda's conversation with Lisa. "I must say, I love your hair colour. Does it run in your family?"

Zelda smiles and giggles, "I'm not sure, my parents don't…"

"Yes, Victoria, it runs in the family. General Williams was a red head," Thomas blurts out, interrupting Zelda.

Lisa and Fiona giggle as Thomas winks playfully at Victoria.

"Why are you laughing? I don't get it," says Zelda.

"Haven't you seen his portraits? He had jet black hair," Fiona explains kindly.

"Bugger off, Thomas, I was only trying to make conversation! I was going to ask about her hair being short," Victoria throws back sharply, trying to save herself embarrassment, but holds his stare bashfully.

Giggling to herself, Zelda replies, "I cut it myself – not that my parents were impressed. My mother was furious and threatened to lock me away until it grew back."

Spencer tries to regain control over the conversation by asking Zelda, "Are you coming to the Wood Saturday afternoon? Or did your parents say no?"

Zelda thinks for a moment, reflecting on what her parents had said and how they warned her not to go. She takes a second to look at her friends. She notices the way they look at her; the admiration. She considers her time spent in Hopewood and how the people around her seem to hang on to every word she speaks. The rebellious temptation to explore is too irresistible. "Sure. Sounds great."

"We'll make sure the Hopewood monster doesn't get you!" says Thomas, trying to scare an excited Zelda with a grin on his face.

"Monster? What monster?" asks Zelda, feigning ignorance.

"You haven't heard about the Hopewood Monster?" Fiona says in a surprised tone. "Tell her, Spencer," she adds, folding her arms.

"About fifteen years ago, my father said one of the Adams' kids – he was about twelve years old, the same as us – ran away because he was tortured and tormented by some of the townsfolk and he went to live in the Wood but he has never been seen since. Some say he was sent away because he was disturbed but there are lots of rumours going around… I even heard he was driven out by the locals because he didn't look like you or I and that he was dumb and he attacked someone but that's only if you want to believe them," Spencer explains sinisterly.

"Well, tell her about the things that have gone missing! And the hooded figure!" Victoria urges.

"Well… apparently, some unexplained things have gone missing over time – tools, a wheel, etcetera – and some people have said they've seen a hooded figure lurking in the shadows around the town at dusk or dawn. Some reckon that he tries to see his parents," continues Spencer.

Lisa jumps in. "It's a load of nonsense," she says, trying

to defuse the tension. "She won't want to live here if you carry on!" she adds.

Spencer chimes in, saying, "That's only if you want to believe the local stories. I've been all over the Wood and have never seen anything or anyone in there so I wouldn't worry."

"Local folklore and silly stories," says Zelda dismissively.

Thomas approaches Zelda from behind and, while looking in Victoria's direction, he puts his hands on Zelda's shoulders and says playfully to her, "He'll come and get you."

Zelda steps forward to pull away from Thomas, turns to face him and says, "I'm sure I'll be fine."

"Speaking of silly stories, what's the story behind monkey hangers? That's what people are called where you're from, right, Zelda?" asks Spencer.

"Well, the story goes that during the Napoleonic Wars, a French ship was wrecked in a storm off the coast of Hartlepool. The only survivor from the ship was a monkey, allegedly dressed in a French sailor uniform – Captain's pet, I guess. On finding the monkey on the beach, some locals decided to hold an impromptu trial and since the monkey was unable to answer their questions (and because they had seen neither a monkey nor a Frenchman before), they concluded that the monkey must be French. And a spy. It was found guilty. Something like that," says Zelda.

"Well, what happened to the monkey?" asks Victoria.

"It was sentenced to death and hanged on the beach," says Zelda giggling.

"I don't know whether to laugh or cry," says Spencer.

Fiona says giggling, "Come on. We best be getting home. It's getting late."

As the sun sets low in the sky, they start to walk back home together and, one by one, they break off from the group. Soon, it's just Fiona and Zelda walking together linked arm in arm.

Zelda asks Fiona, "You don't think there's a monster in the Wood or a hooded figure lurking about, do you?"

Fiona replies, "No. Course not."

In that moment, they hear a noise behind them. They both glance around in the direction of the noise but see nothing. Fiona and Zelda look each other in the eye in shock but burst out laughing and hurry home.

Zelda's first week had flown. She settled in nicely with her new group of friends. Saturday soon arrives and Zelda is thinking of how she can go to the Wood with the others. After pondering for a few minutes, she thinks she may have an idea. She would offer to help her parents with some extra chores and ask to go to the common once again. Once there she could venture just a bit further and into the Wood.

Zelda whizzes through her chores quickly and after asking her parents about the common, which they reluctantly agree to, she changes clothes and slides in her favourite hair clips with a black horse on them (they stand out against her beautiful red hair) and then knocks for Fiona.

They head down to the common to meet the others

who are already waiting and all are wearing old clothes and hats. Victoria and Lisa have satchels hanging off their hips and the boys have homemade rucksacks. They all head off towards the Wood, two by two, laughing and joking and larking about.

Thomas asks Spencer, "What's that handle sticking out of your backpack?"

Spencer reaches his right hand over his right shoulder, grabs the handle and pulls out a large machete.

"What? This?" replies Spencer, showing the big machete off with a smirk.

"Woah! Where did you get that?" asks Thomas.

"It's my father's. It'll make getting through the Wood easier," replies Spencer.

"Does he know you have it?" shouts Victoria from behind.

Turning his head to the side to answer, Spencer shouts, "No! Of course not. And he's not going to find out. I'll put it back before he notices."

"You can keep it away from me!" shouts Lisa.

Stepping inside the Wood, Spencer puts the machete to work by clearing a path (and to test its sharpness). They slowly make their way deeper and deeper into the Wood, swishing and slicing the machete.

"It's good fun," says Spencer. Swinging and chopping away, he chops thicker and thicker branches, until THUD! The machete gets jammed in a branch.

"Ha, looks like Spencer has met his match. Tree… one. Spencer… zero," says Victoria jokingly.

They all spread out, ducking under branches and stepping over logs. Zelda catches something out the corner of her eye. It seems to be dark, shadowy and moving slowly. Standing still, she tries to see if she can make out what it is. Zelda looks around the area to make sense of what it could be. Suddenly, she realises the group has left her behind.

She makes her way through the Wood to catch up with the others and then she hears Lisa shouting back to her, "Come on, Zelda!"

As Zelda moves through the Wood, the same dark shadowy thing in the distance holds her attention. She looks hard, and after staring for a minute, she's taken aback to realise that she is looking at a pair of eyes… then they blink. Human eyes. Her heart starts beating hard and fast. The dark shadowy thing disappears back into the undergrowth. She fixes her attention in the same direction, noticing the odd plant moving or low branch flick back into place. Her curiosity compels her to follow.

The others slowly make their way through the Wood and they roam the between the trees. Lisa, who is lagging at the back of the group a few metres away from Victoria, looks behind and realises that she can't see Zelda anymore.

"Zelda?" Lisa shouts and stares in the direction where she thought Zelda was. "Victoria, can you see Zelda?"

Victoria stops, looks at Lisa to see if she seems serious, and then looks back into the Woods.

After looking around for any signs of Zelda, Victoria shouts at the others. "Can any of you see Zelda anywhere?"

The rest of them stop and look around for her.

"She can't be that hard to spot. She has bright red hair!" says Thomas, laughing uncertainly.

"She must have gone back to town. It's darker in the Wood. Maybe she doesn't like the dark? Maybe we scared her with the ghost stories? She's probably gone home and didn't want to admit it," says Spencer, making sense of the situation. "She'll be fine. She can't have been far from the Wood's edge so she didn't have far to go and we'll catch up with her once we get back," Spencer continues.

"Besides, we don't have far to go. We're only going a little further," adds Thomas.

They continue to the spot they usually go to.

Zelda, still intent on sneaking up on her mystery prey, feels the undergrowth thickening beneath her feet the further she explores. Making her way through the Wood is proving to be more difficult than she thought. As she takes her next step, the loud crack of a branch underfoot pulls her out of her hypnotic trance. Alone. Quiet. She doesn't know where she is. The more she looks around, the more disorientated she feels. She can't figure out which way to the town nor which way the others had left and her heart rate triples.

Zelda closes her eyes for a moment, leans against a tree and takes a deep breath to calm herself down. She can feel the gradual sway of the trunk and its gentle groan created by the wind. Her curiosity is still getting the better of her and, after taking a moment to rest, she continues to look for the creature. She can feel the air getting slightly colder, she feels nervous and her heart starts to beat faster again.

As she continues, the Wood becomes more and more dense. Making her way through, she suddenly notices a faint smell of burning. She looks up and in the distance, she can see a slight trail of smoke rising. It is so very slight that it is almost difficult to see. Moving forward slowly, she finds herself in front of a fence made up of trees and bushes with branches woven in between them. Walking along the fence line, she looks for an opening to wiggle through. She meets a small gap between a tree and some bushes and pushes her body through, scratching her cheek and hands.

Zelda dusts herself down and looks around… what she sees makes her jaw drop in shock.

CHAPTER 4

There, before her, is a rudimentary log cabin. Each log has large patches where the bark is missing. Mud is packed in the crevices with moss covering it in parts. The windows are made up of stacked bottles in different colours, encased in a mud and moss frame.

Zelda notices a white mist creeping in over the area. She walks around the cabin which is lashed together with cordage. With each footstep, her heart beats faster. She cautiously makes her way around the exterior of the cabin. Her breathing becomes faster and deeper and her mouth is dry, small beads of sweat start to form on her brow. She looks all around to see any signs of movement.

As she moves around to the front of the cabin, she sees an even bigger window aside a rather average-looking green front door. 'The door must have come from town,' she thinks, 'it has the number nineteen on it. How strange.' The door is made to a high standard of precision and the paint is immaculate – rather at odds with the home-made rustic feel of the cabin. Underneath the number, someone has delicately carved the word 'Homewood' next to a little square of green-tinted glass in the top centre. At waist height, a black wrought iron knob and matching letterbox juts out from the wood.

Approaching the door slowly and cautiously, her heart

still pounding, she knocks gently. The eerie silence from the Wood makes the knock echo through the trees. After a few moments, she reaches for the handle, twists the knob and pushes gently.

The door opens slowly with a creak. The dim light from the windows creates a multicoloured haze. A small fire burns gently in a corner, smoke slithering and disappearing into a hole that has been hacked into the corner wall. The base is made from layered stones with smouldering logs on top. A log-frame bed sits in the other corner. Leaves quilted between old rags and bits of cotton are interlocked to create a mattress, draped with numerous blankets. A simple stool made from woven branches sits adjacent to the bed next to a small table made from a log stump. On the table's surface lays a thick chunky board with an oil lamp resting on top. A collection of little figures of animals and people all sit above the table on the windowsill near a beautiful box tucked neatly in the corner.

Zelda takes tiny footsteps towards the box, wanting to see it up close. She approaches the windowsill and takes a hold of the box. It is handcrafted with a scene of the town and has the word 'Homewood' written across it but the letter M looks like it was etched to replace the letter P. This small detail doesn't mar its beauty but adds extra character. Zelda is transfixed by its elegance and design – she has never seen anything so beautiful!

Just as she is admiringly moving her finger over the surface, two thuds of heavy feet sound suddenly at the doorway. Zelda freezes with fear. She can hear heavy deep breathing and pungent smell of earth and sweat.

The box slips out of Zelda's trembling hands.

"NOOO!" shouts Joseph in a deep rough voice. He lunges forward towards Zelda to save the box and she turns to face the tall shrouded stranger.

As Joseph charges forward, his heavyset shoulder slams into Zelda. She hits the wall of the cabin with an awkward wallop and falls lifelessly to the floor. Joseph picks the box up and checks for any damage. The lid feels a little loose but intact.

He turns his attention to the body on the floor. There's a small pool of blood emerging from her head. Dropping to his knees, he slides his trembling hand and arm under Zelda's shoulders and lifts her to see her face. Her head hangs back over his arm. His eyes well up with guilt and remorse. Hugging Zelda's body, Joseph strokes her hair and sobs.

The rest of the group head back into town, laughing and joking and in high spirits.

Lisa says, "We should all go to Zelda's house and make sure she got home alright."

"Go on then. We don't want a repeat of what happened to you when we were all playing hide and seek and no one could find you," says Thomas laughing. "I still remember when the whole street was out looking for you. And you! You were asleep under your bed the whole time," he chuckles.

They all laugh the rest of the way to Zelda's house. Victoria knocks on the door a few times with her knuckles clenched into a fist. A few seconds pass and they can hear the voices of Mr and Mrs Williams.

Spencer looks at Thomas, then Victoria, and their faces change to worry.

"What's wrong with you lot?" asks Lisa.

"We can only hear the voices of her parents and not Zelda," says Spencer.

They all start to become anxious just as the door opens and Mrs Williams greets them.

"Hello, children! Oh, why the worried faces?" she says with a smile. "Where is Zelda?"

"Well, that's the thing. We thought she was here," says Thomas.

"Why would she be here? She said she was going to the common with you lot," says Esme.

"What? We went to the Wood and when she didn't keep up with us, we thought she just came home," says Spencer. "But that was hours ago," he adds.

At that moment, realisation sets in for everyone.

"Oh my merciful heavens," says Esme in a concerned voice. "Robert! Robert! Come quick!"

Within seconds, Zelda's father, a smartly dressed man with a waistcoat and tie, is at the door and says, "Yes? What is it?"

"It's Zelda. She went into the Wood, even though we told her not to," says Esme.

The news of her not being allowed to go shocks all of

the children. With that, Robert goes back in the house and immediately returns tieless and with his coat on.

"We didn't know, Mrs Williams. Honest," says Spencer.

"Of course you didn't know. Zelda wouldn't tell you what she couldn't do, only what she can. Zelda does what Zelda wants," says Esme in disgust.

"I'll organise a search party. You stay here in case she comes home," says Robert.

In short time, Robert secures the help of twenty people from the local streets – five of them being the children's fathers. The five children persuade the adults to let them join the search as they were with her last. The sun is setting low in the sky. Armed with long hiking sticks, hay forks and oil lamps, they set off into the Wood.

In no time at all, they reach the area and without hesitation, Robert says loudly, "Everyone, spread out! If we form a line of, say, a few yards apart and that way we should search more effectively."

Like soldiers following orders, they form a line and immediately start searching.

"Be careful, Zelda may be laid anywhere," shouts Robert.

As they're searching the Wood, the remaining sunlight fades into spikes of light flickering through the trees. Slowly, the Wood is transformed into a visual fortress.

Spencer says to Thomas, "The Wood seems a lot different when it's getting dark."

As the search moves on, Robert feels a growing sense

of frustration and mulls things over in his mind: the recent arguments at home and Zelda's defiant actions. Then his frustration turns into desperation and his love for his daughter. He begins to shout, "Zelda! Zelda!"

The others copy him. They slowly make their way through the Wood. It is almost pitch black and the spikes of light slowly fade into darkness. The oil lamps are shining in a row as if suspended on an invisible wire hanging like fireflies stuck on branches and are moving like the wind is playing with them. Suddenly a loud yell of pain bellows from Fiona's father. He has badly hurt his ankle and is unable to walk on it. The group gradually surround him and Robert provides first aid.

"We must make a stretcher and take him back. We'll have to continue first thing in the morning," Robert says.

On returning to the town, Robert is feeling angry, frustrated and upset that the search didn't go as planned. 'How do I explain that I couldn't find her? I'm her Dad. I have let her down!' He slows his pace to a stumble and stops alongside a wooden cart and leans his back against it. His feelings build fast into a force of blind panic and it possesses his body. He holds his search stick horizontally with both hands and immediately breaks it over his knee. He drops the bent and fractured stick on the floor and stares at his roughened and slightly bruised hands. He re-clenches his hands into fists and squeezes them with all his might, eventually giving out a primal yawp.

As he returns home, he hopes to see Zelda sitting at

the kitchen table awaiting his return and that the long, arduous search was all for nothing. His heart flutters as he approaches the house, holding on to optimistic thoughts. Esme throws the door open almost immediately with a hopeful look on her face. Seeing Robert by himself, she collapses to the floor and wails into her hands. Robert helps Esme up. They close the door and they go in.

"I'm sorry we couldn't find her, but the Wood was very difficult to search through," says Robert, thinking that he has let Esme and Zelda down. "We will start again first thing in the morning. I promise," he adds while weeping and hugging Esme.

The next day, Robert is quick to reorganise the search party again with a few more people – all except for Fiona's father. They decide to ask the five children for clues or a better understanding of what may have happened. Leaving the children behind, they head off to the Wood.

After searching, and searching, and searching and a full day of exploration, they are tired, hungry and exhausted. They head back to town again, defeated, with still no sign of Zelda. Day after day, they continue to extensively look but Zelda is nowhere to be seen. Over the next few days, fewer and fewer people help with the search, until the search gradually comes to an end, much to Robert and Esme's frustration.

An entire week passes when Esme is sat pondering in the house over a cup of tea and decides to go for a walk to help clear her head as it is a fresh morning. She strolls down Hawkes

Lane towards the high street, takes in her surroundings and listens to the bird song when it is interrupted by wooden tapping noises coming from the carpenter's workshop. She wanders over to take a closer look. The large entrance door is open enough to just walk in.

Esme can see William working at his workbench using his mallet and chisel, so she gives a little cough to make her presence known to him.

Realising someone is in the workshop, William downs his tools and says, "Good morning."

"Good morning," she replies, while looking around his workshop at the various cabinets, picture frames and projects, admiring his craftsmanship. "You have a fantastic eye for detail, Mr Wood," she adds.

"Thank you. That's very kind of you to say," he says.

"Is this all your work or do you have people working for you?" she asks.

"No, it's all my work. I nearly had an apprentice once," he says, smiling with fond memories.

"Nearly?" she asks.

"Yes. There was this one boy called Joseph who used to help me regularly. I think it helped him to get away from the other children," he says.

Esme looks at him with a frown, expecting him to elaborate.

"The other children made his life very difficult sometimes. You see, he didn't look like the rest of us and, well, children can be cruel. I'm sure you've heard the stories," he continues.

At that moment, Esme realises he was referring to the boy who ran away. Memories race through her mind about Zelda. A sullen look engulfs her face and her eyes well up. Esme says, "Sorry I have to go." Her hand flies to soothe her quivering bottom lip. Making her excuses, she leaves.

"Sorry, I didn't mean to upset you," shouts William after her.

Walking along the street away from the workshop, Esme mulls over the recent move and Zelda's disappearance. She tries to make sense of everything and, without even realising her destination, she is standing at the edge of the Wood – the closest she has ever been to it. She looks through the trees at the rays of light shining through at different angles. The more she looks, the more she stares and thinks, 'My daughter is in there.' Her heart races a little as she becomes flustered.

The wind picks up and blows Esme's hair and the more she stares into the Wood, the more her emotions climb. The wind howls, murmurs and moans with creeping and rustling noises as it swirls around. Esme's eyes widen when she is convinced she hears, "Mother," in a susurrate of wind. With her adrenaline pumping and without caring about her expensive new blue dress snagging on branches or getting filthy, Esme shouts into the Wood, "I'm coming, Zelda!"

With a great sense of determination, she steps into the thick mass of trees and shrubbery. Esme climbs through as best as she can. The boots she is wearing help but the skirt of her dress catches on various stumps and broken branches. With the same will power as Zelda, she fights her way through, her dress progressively ruined with rips and dirt.

Sliding off a large smooth log, she stands for a minute to catch her breath. Her arm outstretched, she leans against a tree. Her mind still in race mode, her adrenaline pumping and her heart beating heavily, she continues, disoriented with no real sense of direction.

Every direction, whichever way she turns, looks the same. Esme smells a whiff of smoke. She looks left... she looks right... back and forth. Darkness. As she moves through the Wood, the smell strengthens. Then, in front, she can see a clear line of smoke. She makes her way towards it, cautiously. Suddenly, she comes across what looks like a natural fence line made with trees and bushes and branches woven in between.

After a little searching, Esme finds a gap and forces her way through, ripping her skirt again. She grabs the the skirt and with a sharp pull, rips the loose parts away. Esme stands upright to collect her thoughts and is stunned to find that there, in front of her, is a rustic log cabin with stacked bottles for windows. She surveys the area and walks around to find a door. She approaches a dark green door with the number nineteen on it and 'Homewood' carved underneath. She knocks gently and pushes it open.

Once inside, she looks around to find a makeshift bed and a fireplace made out of different sized rocks, and notices something on the floor: a hair clip with a black horse on it.

At that moment, Joseph steps inside.

Esme, only thinking the worst, launches a frenzied attack which only a mother can understand. Esme gives the fight of her life, throwing punch after punch. With outstretched arms, Joseph defensively grapples with her upper arms. Adrenaline pumping, she musters the strength of ten men and whips her arm down and back (which released his grip) then clenches her fist and throws it over her head like a clock on fast forward and she hits out.

Joseph releases his grip before falling to the ground. Esme continues her crazed, punch-after-punch attack on Joseph as he is laid on the floor. His arms are the only source of his protection. His legs are in the air, bent at the knee ready to defend himself, recoiled and ready to kick out at any approach.

Under an onslaught of attacks, also in the fight of his life, in panic mode and screaming through fits of terror, he breathlessly cries, "No," and, "Get out!"

The punches still fly. Leaning closer to Joseph, she balances on her tip toes and, about to fall, she stands upright to regain her balance.

Joseph fights through internal panic and seizes his opportunity... he kicks out with full force.

Esme's body lands slumped against the logged wall.

Her face is covered in scratches, bruises and she has a bloody nose, and she is exhausted after having the wind heavily knocked out of her. Her eyes roll back and her eyelids close. She tries to get her breath back as Joseph struggles up to his feet with his back to her.

He holds his hand against the side of his head as he struggles to regain his balance and understand what is going on. He turns around. His face is scratched and bruised. Looking down at what seems like a lifeless body, he moves to grab it and drag it outside. He no sooner grabs the clothing about the neckline when at that moment, Esme's eyes open wide (and as if life itself pauses), she grabs a stone from the fireplace and smashes it into Joseph's head.

With a great thud, Joseph collapses.

As Esme rests for a moment to catch her breath, there is suddenly a figure standing in the doorway. Esme squints but is finding it difficult to focus and has a slight ringing in her ears from the bang to her head.

She hears, "Oh my God! MOTHER!"

With a trembling chin and quivering lip, a tear falls from each eye. Esme looks around in all directions for the very familiar voice and tries to comprehend the one word she thought she would never hear again. The figure moves in front of Esme and a gentle hand touches her face. Her eyes come into focus and there, in front of her, is Zelda.

They embrace tightly and cry with such sweet relief,

both mother and daughter saying sorry for what the other had been through.

Zelda helps her mother up onto a stool. "How...? What...? Where have you been? We've been worried sick," says a very confused but euphoric Esme.

"We'll get you cleaned up and sort things out and I'll try to explain everything," answers Zelda. "I really am sorry. I know you both must have been worried and I should have tried to come home sooner to you."

"I'm honestly just so relieved you're alive and in one piece! How awful! To have suffered being cooped up in such a dingy place with such an awful creature of a man," an emotional Esme replies.

Then, with the help of her mother, they place Joseph onto the bed and clean his face. Zelda turns her attention to her mother. Sitting her down, she gradually cleans up her mother's face and starts at the beginning.

"The day I left for the common, we came into the Wood and I got distracted by something out of the corner of my eye. I decided to follow it out of curiosity," says Zelda.

Her mother looks at her in such wonder and her face reveals a variety of emotions as Zelda explains

"When I realised I was distracted, I looked around for the others but couldn't see or hear them. Before I knew it, I was confused as to where I was. I came across this cabin. Once inside, I found that box on the windowsill." Zelda points at the beautiful box still in its place. "Joseph then came in and my hands started shaking and I dropped the box. He tried to save it and lunged towards me and his shoulder hit me. I hit the wall and passed out." Zelda continues.

Esme gives a disapproving look at Joseph but Zelda stops her by reaching her arm out and places her hand on her mother's hand for reassurance.

"Don't hurt him, mother. He saved me. I was asleep for days and unable to walk for a few more but he helped me," she explains. "He told me of how he ended up here – how everyone made his life horrible and how they bullied him. They even called him the work of the devil," says Zelda with a sympathetic look on her face. "And I know how that feels after my last school. So we helped each other, really."

Zelda grabs her mother's hand and grips it tightly, leans forward and kisses it. Zelda's eyes fill up with tears. They both stand and tightly hug each other.

"I'm so sorry, mother," says a relieved Zelda.

Esme looks down at Joseph and feels guilty and remorseful after everything that had happened; she thinks to herself how easy it is for one to jump to conclusions and to label people over superficial appearances and small minded superstition.

After a few hours, Joseph stirs and moans with pain.

Zelda comforts and explains everything to a confused and anxious Joseph.

While the three of them are chatting away, Esme makes a bold suggestion. "Why don't you come back to the town with us? I'm sure things will be different now."

Joseph thinks about it for a little while and looks around at the cabin and while he looks around, he stares into space with a blank look on his face. The memories from the past race through his mind. His head drops slowly forward, he folds his arms and his body begins to shake nervously at the very thought of returning.

"No, I don't want to," he says softly.

Zelda, seeing him visibly shaken, slips from the chair and sits on the floor in front of him.

"Sorry, I didn't mean to upset you," she says sympathetically. She places her hand on his cheek and lifts his head.

A single tear rolls down the side of his nose and he gives her a little grin.

"I like it here. The animals are never mean to me and I feel safe here," replies Joseph.

"Yes, I understand that," says Zelda. She pauses for a moment, with her hand touching her chin and bottom lip as she's working out the best way to speak her mind. "Sometimes there are times when we need to be brave if we want to change something, help someone or make a situation better," Zelda explains.

Joseph shrugs his shoulders.

Zelda continues, "I had to be brave at my old school and stand up to bullies. My mother was brave moving here, so far away from her home and family. I think if you are brave enough to build all this and live here for all this time, I think you could be just as brave to return to town. We would help you."

"I don't know," Joseph mumbles into his sleeve.

"I know it must feel very difficult but I think you are strong and amazing and the bravest person I've ever met. And surely not everyone was so mean. There must have been at least one person you thought was your friend, before."

"There was, actually. He was my greatest friend. He still is." Joseph stares into space for a moment. "And you really mean you'll help me?"

"Yes. Absolutely!" answers a nodding Zelda.

He bites his lip and ponders. "Well, all right, then," he nods.

CHAPTER 5

They make their way through the Wood, helping each other past the debris and trunks extending across the woodland floor. They no sooner reach the edge of town when people realise who it is and they stare and gawk.

Word spreads rapidly, faster than a gust of wind.

As they arrive at the main square, they're slowly surrounded and people clap and cheer while others are jeering. Popping out of the gathered crowd at different places are five familiar faces: Fiona, Spencer, Thomas, Lisa and Victoria. They all hug with joy and relief at seeing Zelda again.

"What's going on? Did the monster hurt you?" Spencer says, nodding in the direction of Joseph, trying to find out what has happened.

"No, he's really nothing bad at all. In fact, he's kind-hearted and misunderstood. I think that it's this town that's monstrous, and some people need to change and give others a chance," says Zelda with her chin held high.

Robert is quick to arrive at a main square which is bustling with commotion. Looking shabby, pale and rough around his face like he has not slept for days, he greets a filthy Esme. As they share a loving embrace, they are soon joined by Zelda who wraps an arm around each parent and grabs them tightly. The taunting and jeering from the crowd grows louder and a very shy Joseph can only stand in silence, dressed in badly fitted clothes, with shoulder length rough hair and a patchy beard.

The chaos leaves Joseph lost for words. The people part when seemingly out of nowhere, William appears. He immediately greets Joseph and, once Joseph recognises William, they hug tightly like their lives depend on it.

The jeering from the crowd increases.

William is quick to Joseph's defence by turning around and standing in front of him defensively.

Robert senses the unrest and shouts to the rabble, "People of Hopewood, some of you know who I am. My name is Dr Williams and I have only recently moved here with my wife, Esme, and daughter, Zelda. Please, let us have calm. I'm aware you're all concerned and uneasy because this man you all know to be Joseph has returned, but I can assure you there is nothing to fear."

But the crowd continue to shout and jeer.

Zelda tugs her father's jacket for his attention and says, "May I try?"

Then, with loving eyes, Robert grabs Zelda at the waist and lifts her onto his shoulder.

"My name is Zelda and I want you all to know that Joseph isn't the evil, demonised person you have all come to fear." Zelda looks over at some of the people who were jeering while William places his hand on Joseph's shoulder for support. "I may have died if it wasn't for Joseph's help. He may seem to be different and may not talk the same but I was hurt in the Wood and he helped me. We need to find it in ourselves and in our hearts to be more accepting and understanding," she proclaims.

The crowd look around between themselves, chattering. A sound of clapping grows louder from Victoria, Lisa, Spencer, Thomas and Fiona. It spreads through the crowd like wildfire and is followed by cheering and the shouting of 'Hear, hear!,' and 'Indeed.'

As the crowd disperses, Robert places his hand on Joseph's shoulder and says, "I think you need a quick examination just to make sure you're well."

William, Joseph and Robert, closely followed by Esme and Zelda arm in arm, make their way along Hawkes Lane to the Williams' house. After the examination, Robert leaves Joseph to dress and organise himself, and goes into the next room with Esme and William.

"He's in great shape. He has limited speech and general intelligence but overall, he's in great shape considering he's been living in the Wood for so long," says Robert. He then pauses for a moment and rubs his chin with his hand. "I may be wrong but I think he has a medical condition. I've been hearing about it in some of my professional circles. Joseph definitely has a look of it. But with some help and care and a safe place to stay, I think he'll be just fine," says Robert.

They return to the room to see Joseph.

Esme places her hand gently on Joseph's shoulder and says, "We need to find you somewhere to stay."

After a moment's silence, Joseph replies while looking down at the floor. Feeling out of place, he whispers, "Where's my mother and father? Couldn't I live with them?"

Unsure of what to say, Esme glances over to Robert and then over to William in the hope that one of them will say something. William clenches his fists on his knees, then takes a deep breath as he looks over at Joseph and says, "I'm sorry to have to be the one to tell you. After you left, a few people decided to make up some bad stories about them and the more people decided to believe the lies, the more support they got. In the end, your family left for their own safety and we haven't heard from them since."

Esme comforts an emotional Joseph as his bottom lip starts to tremble.

"You know I've always enjoyed having you around," says William in a breaking deep voice.

Esme and Robert look at each other like they'd both had the same idea when William says, "I have a letter here from your mother that I think you need to read."

Joseph takes a hold of the letter with his mother's familiar handwriting on it and his eyes well up with so many memories that he is unable to speak.

Sensing his difficulty, Esme says softly, "Would you like me to read it to you? If that's fine with you, William?" They both nod in agreement. Esme takes the letter and begins to read…

Dear William,

I've been burdened with a secret for far too long but if it had become known it would have had enormous repercussions. I hope you can find it in your heart one day to forgive me. You have always been a wonderful friend and if Joseph ever returns, I hope you can find it in your heart to look after him and keep him safe... because Joseph is your son.

I was so happy when you took him under your wing. I'm truly sorry for any hurt I've caused you.

My kindest wishes,

Daisy

"We have lots to talk about and catch up on... so how would you like to come and stay with me and help in the workshop... like before," asks William.

Joseph's face lights up and they both hug.

The revelation makes Esme and Robert look at each other with surprised faces and a glint in their eyes like they are reading each other's minds. Zelda is sitting with her hand semi covering her wide open mouth and a face of utter disbelief. A safe place for Joseph to live, help and company for William, and a family for both of them.

Joseph and William make their way to the front door followed by Esme, Robert and Zelda.

Stepping onto the street, they both thank the Williams family for all their help. Zelda looks Joseph in the eye and says with a gentle grin, "Good luck, Joseph."

William and Joseph head off towards the workshop, with lots to talk about to catch up on lost time.

They walk down the street, their lives now heading in the same direction to start a new chapter as a family.

CHAPTER 6

A new sense of calm is in the air. Stepping outside, Joseph wanders over to the stores across the street, accompanied by William who is keeping a watchful eye. They both enjoy each other's company, sharing fun and laughter as they browse the wares in town. They're soon back in the workshop having lunch before starting on another job.

The days follow on in a similar fashion. Joseph is a visibly relaxed character, more polished and presentable, and yet always seems to peek over his shoulder when venturing outside. Every time there is a loud noise, maybe children laughing or the heavy closing of a door, he jumps out of his skin. Sometimes whenever Zelda and the others make their way home from school and they see Joseph about the workshop, they look at each other with a smile of fondness. Occasionally, when the six of them go to the common, Zelda and the others call in to see Joseph and he shows them his current projects.

Leaf by fallen leaf, Autumn is creeping through the town, when one particular morning resists the cold months to come, crisp and sunny and the last dying breath of the summer passing. Joseph visits the baker's shop to buy bread.

Stepping onto the dirt-lined road with his bread under his arm, Joseph looks up the street towards the main square, noticing a small group of young men staring at him. They only stare, until they notice Joseph staring back. And then they point and talk behind their hands to each other, eyeing Joseph.

Looking at the ground, he retreats to the workshop. Back against the door, locked and bolted, he rebels against his pounding heart and swallows back the nausea brewing in his stomach.

"I'm safe. I have William. I'm safe. I *am* safe."

Like a dark cloud hanging over his head, the same group of youths lurk around the workshop, or the square, or the common. Each time Joseph steps outside, he can feel their eyes ripping him apart, as if he is a rabbit in the presence of a pack of wild wolves. He crosses over to the other side of the street to avoid them, pretending not to even notice them. Not a single soul on the street, neither Joseph nor his predators, notice William watching from his doorframe with a look of disgust.

The following day William and Joseph are cleaning out the workshop when William asks Joseph to pull the heavy cart outside.

"The room is too cramped. I'm not the tidiest at the best of times and my knees aren't what they used to be," chides William.

Joseph opens the large workshop doors and firmly grabs the T-bar handle to pull it outside with relative ease. With a grin on his face, he thinks to himself, 'Either I'm stronger, or the cart is lighter than I remember.' Walking backwards and trying to steer at the same time is still as tricky as it ever was. He moves over to the left, crossing his feet and trying not to trip, and then to the right. Concentrating on his feet crossing again, he stumbles backwards on a small stone, feeling an abrupt thud against his back.

"Bloody hell!"

Although he is quick to stand upright to stop the cart, he trips over his words, scrambling together an apology to the stranger he bumped into. After turning around, he arrives face to face with one of the young men who is flanked by the other three, clad in rough and ragged clothes with dirt on their faces and scruffy unbrushed hair.

As they stand there, nose to nose, Joseph can feel the stale breath blowing across his cheek. He steps to one side and says, "Sorry."

"You should have stayed gone, you freak!" the stranger retorts with a screwed up face, head tilting forward and eyes fixed on Joseph.

Joseph, trying not to be intimidat, attempts to manoeuvre the cart but his path is cut off by the other lads. One grasps his shoulder to hold him fast, while the other two secure the cart and cover any chance of escape. The gang leader spins Joseph around.

"I'm going to make you sorry you came back," hisses the leader, clenching his hands. He twists his body, steps back and swings his fist towards a wincing Joseph, who leans back and avoids it. The leader, even more enraged, is quick to throw another fist.

Joseph's instinctual reaction is to block the impact and catches their fist at the wrist, which stuns the gang.

"I'm not the scared boy everyone remembers," shouts Joseph.

His heart is racing and his adrenaline is pumping.

Hearing raised voices outside, William steps out of the workshop and sees the commotion in the street.

"Hey," he shouts. "Leave him alone!"

The leader whips his hand out of Joseph's grasp, rubs his wrist and says, "It's not over – this isn't finished!"

All four of them storm away, leaving Joseph and William trying to understand what happened. They both return to the workshop to finish tidying up.

"Are you alright?" asks William.

"Yes, I'm fine," replies a shaken Joseph. "Who was that?"

"David the miller's son and his friends. They live on the other side of town," replies William.

At that moment, he remembers David's father was part of the mob with pitchforks, who forced Joseph's parents to leave. The thought leaves a lump in William's throat.

It is Saturday afternoon and both Joseph and William are hard at work when Joseph says, "After we finish this, can we go for a walk around the shops and to the main square, please?"

"Well, sure. But I have one or two little jobs to do, first. If you want to, you can go out yourself for a wander and when I'm finished I'll meet you. Remember, we still need to go to the Wood later to chop down a tree for another job," says William.

"Thanks. I can't wait," Joseph smiles broadly to William with genuine excitement.

Joseph, out the door and into the chilly morning, wanders around the high street, looking at the various goods in the shop windows. He casually walks around the main square and enjoys seeing the hustle and bustle, before retracing his route back down the high street.

As he saunters along, his mind is caught by the roof tops and the birds flying in the sky – it never fails to capture his imagination. He is suddenly snapped out of his daydream by a familiar voice.

"Joseph!" shouts Zelda to get his attention.

He looks over to see Zelda and the others hanging out on the common. He greets them with a big grin. They all gather round him, laughing, joking and basking in each other's company. Suddenly, the cheerful atmosphere is thrown into disarray as Joseph turns to see four shabbily dressed young men heading their way. They have weapons and menacing looks on their faces.

Fiona is beside him and as she sees them, she covers her mouth, her eyes widen and she gasps, "Oh my goodness!"

As the rest of the group look, their faces are an assortment of shock, despair and terror.

Zelda is quick to Joseph's defence. "Don't worry. We'll help you," she says, putting her fists up by her face like a boxer.

Spencer warns her, "Zelda, this isn't the time for a fight. That's David, the miller's son. He has an *evil* reputation."

Thomas sticks his two penn'orths in. "I say let's get out of here!" He no sooner speaks when the four young men spread themselves evenly across the street as if trying to corner an animal.

Joseph falls into panic mode and a look of terror engulfs his face.

Victoria is quick with a solution. "Joseph, we know you're scared," she says. "You head into the Wood and if you go and hide in the cabin, we'll tell William what's happened and where you are."

The four men are inching closer but Joseph is frozen with fear, so Zelda, Spencer and Thomas push him in the direction of the Wood and shout, "Joseph, run!"

Realising he has little choice, he hotfoots across the common and into the Wood when David shouts and points to the men on the flanks, "After him."

As Joseph ploughs through the trees and heavy vegetation, a sense of calm rises within him. It almost feels like a game to him as he climbs, jumps and negotiates the jungle-like terrain. The scent of timber sends his pulse racing, and the gust of wind whispers in his ears 'Welcome back…' and 'We missed you.'

Under different circumstances, Joseph would perhaps

laugh and even feel carefree enough to entwine his limbs with the loving arms of his Wood once again. He's almost forgotten how good the Wood made him feel and he embraces the freedom and joy it provides – he feels at home. Suddenly there's a loud shout from behind him.

"Joseph, you can run but you can't hide."

He turns around to survey the area and sees two out in front and David and his best friend behind, barking orders at the other two.

As Joseph continues to move through the Wood, he remembers his idea of hide and seek. One minute he's there, the next he's gone.

"Spread out! Spread out!" come the orders.

"He's here somewhere, find him!"

Zelda, Spencer, Victoria, Thomas, Lisa and Fiona scurry up the high street towards the workshop. As they reach it, the big heavy ornate door swings open and William emerges pulling the cart ladened with an axe, rope and other tools.

Spencer is first to speak up, "Mr Wood! David and his gang have chased after Joseph!"

"I said to go and hide in the cabin in the Wood, so you would know where he is," says Victoria.

Without hesitation, he replies, "Thank you, everyone. Now, let me deal with it. We don't need anyone else getting hurt." As he sharply ushers them away, he stands upright and takes a deep breath to compose himself, squeezes his eyes shut and runs his hand though his hair.

'Somehow, I just knew something like this would happen!' He begins to pull the cart again, only this time like he's in a race.

As they watch him pull the cart down the street, Victoria and Thomas say together, "I think we should go and tell our parents."

Joseph crawls around the floor of the Wood, popping his head up to take a peek at where the men are. He finds a club-shaped branch when an interesting thought occurs to him. One of the ruffians draws closer. Joseph moves amongst the undergrowth and through the gaps created by felled trees, leans against another tree as his heart pounds heavier by the second... he waits.

He makes a conscious effort to steady his breathing, takes another quick look before disappearing again into the undergrowth. He mimes, firmly gripping the stick: one... two... three. Joseph's target is so close now, his breath swirls visibly in the open air. His feet are within arm's reach.

"ARGH!" Joseph screams a battle cry, jumps to stand face to face, and *whack*! The man shrieks a blood curdling shriek and paws at his shin like a wounded animal.

Joseph swings the club again... *thump*!

Over the sobbing and whimpering, he wastes little effort on stealth when he stands and lands a hit across the back. He watches the hulk of the man collapse to the ground and all crying stops dead. Dropping the club, Joseph scrambles for a thick patch of moss and scoops a pile of twigs and soil under the sleeping man's head. No blood, steady breaths.

Vanishing back into the vegetation, and peeking his head up from time to time, he works his way across to where the next gang member.

David and his thugs shout, "Keep looking. He's here, somewhere," and "We're going to get you, monster!"

David climbs over a large log and his feet slip, landing with a thud on his backside. Climbing back to his feet, grabbing the loose rock he slipped on, he thinks in a fit of rage, 'If I see him, I'm going to launch this at his head.'

Joseph stealthily places himself into position again, hiding behind another tree. He dips his head ever so slightly to catch a glimpse of his next target, more bouncy and raring to go than his predecessor.

Weaponless and running out of time, Joseph scans his eyes desperately searching for a solution when a stroke of pure genius strikes! But as Joseph draws back a thick flexible branch achingly slowly, the sound alerts the prowling thug.

"I've got you, now, you filthy urchin." The thug turns towards the mysterious noise.

One… two… three…

"ARGH!" Joseph releases the branch and sends the man flying into another tree, knocking him unconscious to the ground.

Joseph's jaw hits the floor. "Wow."

Too stunned at the impact of his battle tactics, Joseph's observation is immersed on his triumph, rather than his surroundings until it is too late. Seemingly out of nowhere, he feels a sharp and heavy thump on his shoulder, followed by an intense pain. Clenching his shoulder with his hand, he turns, aghast, to see David about fifteen paces away, looking straight at him.

"Missed!" shouts David. "That was meant for your head. I'll just have to use my fist."

Joseph does not wait for David to finish his threat. He disappears into the Wood once again, heading straight for his old cabin.

Approaching the cabin area, he follows the bush woven fence line to an opening marked by a split log. Joseph opens the door and steps into the log cabin, surveying the room. The memories of the last fifteen years flood back – memories of salvaging and gathering logs to build the cabin, and collecting the old glass bottles for the windows. He can still smell the burnt ash in the corner. Hearing voices outside, he snatches the few blankets and foliage from his old bed and climbs underneath to hide.

Moments later, the door flies open. Locking his limbs and staying still, his hyperventilating betrays him.

Almost as if the blankets and bedding aren't there, hands grab Joseph, lifting him into the air in one heave.

In the darkness of the hut, David punches Joseph in the jaw, before landing another blow to his stomach.

"Eumph!" Joseph spits blood.

The sparring couple are joined by David's associate who hovers by the doorway.

Dazed, and with clenched fists, Joseph pushes David away, and he stumbles back. Ignoring the verbal assault from the cabin's entrance, Joseph picks up the oil lamp in the corner and slings it at David. It bounces off his shoulder, peppering his face with glass and smashes with a spark in the fireplace. Oil splatters the logged walls.

Joseph staggers over to the back wall when David lobs a stone from the fireplace at him. He ducks in the nick of time and the stone smashes the window and a gust of wind rushes inside. Swirling around the leaves and debris, a tame blue flame ignites a spark that whips up a furnace, climbing the walls. The flames quickly eat at the cordage that ties the logs together.

David lunges forward to finish his assault by punching Joseph hard again and again until he crumbles to the floor.

"You can *burn* here!" David shouts.

A large figure stands in the doorway holding an axe, flinging the door open with a loud bang. The two men spin around instantly as the flames thrash up the fuel-soaked wall and across the ceiling. Their eyes are as wide as saucers and their faces drain of all colour to a pale white as if a demon is waiting to collect them.

"It's about time you two were taught to respect other people," shouts William, who dispenses two heavy punches in quick succession.

Both men slump to the floor.

He throws Joseph's arm around his neck and they stumble out of the cabin which partially collapses. They fall to their knees and take a sharp intake of breath. Smoke spirals into the starry sky.

"Let's go… there's nothing we can do," instructs William.

"No! We can't leave them in there! That'll make us no better than them," splutters Joseph. He drags his exhausted body back into the cabin.

They pull the unconscious bodies out one at a time and pat out any smaller flames dancing on their clothing. Flat out on the ground to catch their breath, they can hear the cabin creeping and groaning as the flames engulf it. The fire turns the night sky into a blazing orange light, coating the Wood with a thick dark blanket of smoke, rising higher and higher.

The cabin caves in, sending a plume of glowing embers up like stars dancing on a black canvas. William and Joseph pick themselves up, dust themselves down, then formulate a plan to move everyone onto the cart. The unconscious bodies are bound at the wrists and ankles, placed carefully on the cart and tied down so they don't fall off if they wake up mid journey.

They both take hold of the steering bar and make their way back. Forlorn, Joseph asks William, "Why don't people like me? I thought coming back with Esme and Zelda… it was supposed to be better!"

William feels a heavy lump form in his throat and fights the tears away by clearing his throat with a grunt. "Lots of people do like you, Joseph. But there's the minority – more naive and ignorant. They lack compassion. When folk don't understand something or someone, it brings out fear. Nasty and violent. Maybe they didn't feel loved or wanted. Maybe nobody cared for them as kids. The reason doesn't matter. What matters is that – and you must remember this – it's not your fault."

They pull the cart along the high street. Greeted by Zelda, Victoria, Lisa, Fiona, Spencer and Thomas running towards them, they all take hold of a different part of the cart and push to help an exhausted pair of men. Arriving at the main square to a gathering crowd (including Esme and Robert), they untie the four young men who are just starting to regain consciousness and are stunned to be surrounded by so many people.

William and Joseph are warmly greeted by lots of people who sympathise upon seeing Joseph's face cut, bloody, covered in soot, and bruises already swelling. He climbs on the cart to declare, "Good people of Hopewood. Why...? Why me? My family? My friends? My life? I never sinned. I've tried to understand you all but I just don't." Joseph speaks with such vehemence a tear rolls down his cheek.

The crowd has an eerie silence, with stunned faces and mouths wide open in disbelief.

"I'm aware of the stories about me but I'm not a monster," he continues, wiping away the tear. "It's folk like these," pointing to the cart and stuttering, "who are the monsters. Why do you allow it? Why is no one doing something? I saw it. Every. Day. I mean, they tried to *kill* me! In church... that's a sin, yes? I want to believe in this town. There has to be some good. Some hope for you all. Otherwise, what? Hell? More hate? I found my friends and family – change can happen. Love and care – this town was built on those things. Do better." Joseph concludes.

A murmur echoes through the crowd and breaks the tension. Another person coughs. A shuffling from within the crowd creeps towards the cart.

Joseph turns his back on a group of men descending on the now conscious thugs in the cart.

William hands over the last criminal to be led away.

"There you go, Constable, take them away."

The police don't hesitate, marching them away.

As people disperse, Joseph turns to William, places his hand on his shoulder, looks into his eyes and says, "Thanks for everything. Let's go home, Dad."

CHAPTER 7

Joseph and William work on a plethora of projects together in the aftermath of the attack. Between the workshop and his living arrangement, Joseph quickly falls back into a satisfying routine William senses a newfound calmness in him.

Sporting a new beard, which Joseph finds helps him blend in, he occasionally strolls around the high street and main square, watching ladies walking along or tending to their children. Memories of his mother flash through his mind.

He reminisces outside of his old empty house, taking a peek inside through the windows, cupping his hands around the sides of his face. Looking in the kitchen or catching glimpses of the old furniture and items left behind quickly turns into long afternoons spent running his fingers over the dusty banister or rummaging through cupboards, like a child engrossed in a treasure trove. Every moth-eaten blanket, mouldy toy or soggy book strikes a newly uncovered memory of good and bad times with his siblings.

Joseph wakes up in his bed in the house he now calls home, adjoining the workshop. A bright ray of sunshine is shining in his eyes. While getting dressed, he notices a folded piece of paper on the shelf of the bedside cabinet. He unfolds it and reads the letter from his mother to William. After a paragraph in, Joseph's eyes well up and he carefully folds the letter up exactly how he found it. He thinks, 'I need to find them.'

Only half dressed, he heads downstairs and into the kitchen where William is sitting enjoying a cup of tea.

"Good morning," William beams.

"Morning." Joseph takes a seat directly opposite and tucks himself in. He immediately places the letter on the table in front of William. "What happened the night they left?"

William, sitting up abruptly, swallows a mouthful of tea. "Ah," he begins. "Well, we got back from the search party. It went on for so long and you had us all worried sick. They would never give up the search, y'know?" he adds as Joseph rests his elbows on the table. "There was a mob. People were waiting outside of the house. And Richard – your father – well, he didn't really have a choice in his position. Do you understand? He left the town to keep your family all safe." William rubs at his chin.

Joseph stares into space.

Sensing something is bothering him, William asks Joseph, "Can you tell me what's wrong, son?"

"You said that nobody has heard from them since. I want to go and look for them," he replies, simply.

"I'm not sure that's such a good idea, Joseph. Nobody knows where they went. And I don't think it would be wise for you to travel by yourself…"

"Why?" snaps Joseph. "I'm big now." He softens, shrugging apologetically.

"But where will you go? They didn't leave or send a forwarding address." William's eyes shut tight and his fingers pinch the bridge of his nose.

"I have to try." Joseph's voice sounds small.

"So tell me, Joseph… How will you look for them? Where will you look?" asks William, gazing at the cold cup of tea.

"I don't know. But I know I at least have to try. You said they would never give up the search for me, so I'm never going to give up looking for them," replies Joseph.

"They would be happy and content knowing you're alive and well. You can't bleedin' well go out there and break your neck in the process! Think what that would do to your poor mother! And me! It's not like I can go with you."

"Well, why not?"

William huffs, "I've got the workshop to run. This shop keeps a roof over my head and tea in my mug. We can't all just run off into the Wood and live on berries, you know? And my knees aren't what they used to be."

"I'm not stupid, you know," Joseph says. "You don't have to talk to me like I don't know things. You just said that my mother would be happy knowing I'm alive and well. But she doesn't know, does she? So how can she be happy? I know that I won't be until she does and I'll do it on my own if I have to!"

The room hushes for a moment and the faint sound of

birds singing from outside quells the tension. William sips at his cold tea, admiring the sunbeam trickling through the kitchen window and dusting light onto a stack of old books sitting on the counter.

"All right, Joseph. You win. How soon do you want to go?" he asks, resigned.

"Tomorrow. First thing." Joseph's face is still red and his jaw clenches tightly.

Joseph meanders down to the common while the sun is still up to share his news. Drinking in the familiar stores and ordinary people, it occurs to him that it will be his last opportunity to absorb every detail: the dirty roof tiles like mismatched teeth smiling at the sky, the young baker's assistant huffing and puffing while unloading the flour from the cart, customers from the haberdashery tucking away new ribbon spools into their purses, the same old honey-coloured mare sniffing at Joseph's hands parked with a carriage by the tailor's shop. Likewise, he thinks to himself, 'I lived in this town for so long and it's like I'm only really seeing it for the first time now.'

Arriving at the common wearing a big smile at the sight of everyone, Zelda and Spencer make a beeline for Joseph while alerting the others who are quick to join them. "It's good to see you, Joseph," exclaims Zelda as Spencer greets him with a friendly slap on the back.

"I've come down to tell you all something important," says Joseph as they all look at him with bated breath. "I'm going away for a while to look for my family."

A moment of silence halts the excited chatter before the children glance at each other.

"Wow! Really?" blurts out Thomas.

"We'll miss you," says Fiona.

"What an adventure!" replies Spencer excitedly.

"We hope you find them, good luck!" answers Victoria thoughtfully.

Zelda quickly hugs Joseph and says, "Stay safe and come back soon," and then gives him a quick kiss on his cheek.

After saying his goodbyes, Joseph heads back up the high street with a spring in his step and as he looks back, he sees Thomas and Spencer play fighting while the girls laugh loudly… only Zelda returns his glance.

The next morning, after eating a hearty breakfast, Joseph ready to go.

William squares up to Joseph, places both hands on his shoulders and looks Joseph directly in his eyes. "Good luck with your search. When you get to where you think they are, ask everyone you see in the street. Youcan ask in the public houses and cafes," explains William.

"Yes, I will. Thanks for all your help," says Joseph.

"Let's get you packed then."

They pack all of Joseph's things into a backpack with baked goods, fruits and canisters of water, when William says, "I'll leave you to finish up and see you downstairs."

He's sipping tea in the kitchen, when Joseph walks in minutes later and sits down with a nervous sigh.

"You don't have to go if you don't actually want to," explains William.

Joseph looks him in the eyes and nods. "Yes, I do."

"Alright then," says William as he pulls out a leather pouch with a drawstring at the top. He unties the top and Joseph can hear the sound of coins. "Then you're going to need this," William says, pouring gold and silver coins into his hand. "These are my life savings – for emergencies. I want you to take some of it with you in case you need anything. I suggest you tie them to the inside of your pants. I may not agree with you going, but you're a man now. If you can live in the Wood for fifteen years then I'm not going to stop you from going. And for Pete's sake, make sure to write to me when you find them, yes?"

Joseph grabs William, and pulling him into a tight embrace, whispers into his ear, "Really, thank you. I love you."

William laughs a little, slapping Joseph's back and kissing his cheek. "Don't be soft. Now, get going while you still have daylight."

Stepping into the street, William and Joseph are greeted by a small group of well wishers – mainly Zelda, her friends and their parents. With a grin and a wave hiding his trepidation, Joseph sets off in the same direction as his parents did years before.

All day he walks along beaten paths, over fields and streams and through little villages, using them to replenish his food and water. On the journey, he asks villagers if they remember his parents, but it is always the same disappointing answer. He spends the first night in a makeshift wooden shelter, pondering his life while looking up at the stars.

The next morning, Joseph continues to trudge with a trekking stick he found. As evening draws in, he passes a lake surrounded by overhanging trees, reeds and various shrubs that poke out of the water, and decides to go for a swim to bathe. He quickly undresses and with a little apprehension, he eases himself gently into the cold water. He finds the water welcoming, soothing his tired muscles. Lost in the moment, he forgets the woes of life and feels free while he gently swims around and ducks his head under the water from time-to-time.

The sound of young ladies giggling in conversation, blissfully unaware of him, strikes panic and he dives head first among the reeds and bushes by the embankment. As he stands in the chilly water, he shivers while observing the ladies, waiting for them to leave. Once they disappear from view, he is quick to climb out and dress as fast as his shivering limbs allow him.

He continues his journey for hours into the unknown until the light fades. Spotting what looks like a disused barn in a corner of a field in the distance, he trudges inside to settle down for his second night away from home. Once inside, he finds a small stack of hay bales and a rather battered metal pan which he places the pan in his bag. 'It's draughty but dry,' he thinks. Then he beds down for the night between the bales of hay.

As he makes himself comfortable, memories of his bed in the Wood, now crumbled to ash and dust, send him drifting into a deep sleep.

BLAM! Joseph's eyes are thrust open as he's rudely woken by the farmer firing a shotgun.

"I don't know who you are," shouts the angry farmer, "but I can hear your snoring! You have two minutes to leave the barn or the next shell will have your name on it."

Joseph jumps up, fumbles around for his bag while his full body shakes with fear. He darts out of the door and runs for his life. He runs as fast as his legs will carry him, his heart racing, too frightened to look back.

As he slows down, miles down the beaten track, he brings himself to a stop and tries to get his breath back. He looks up and daylight is only just, now, starting to creep over the horizon. Then he looks back and is relieved to see there is no angry farmer chasing him. He looks down at his slightly trembling hands as he calms down and the luck of his escape dawns on him. 'I think I've shit my trousers'. After quickly checking the status of his rear end, Joseph wipes the sleep from his eyes and carries on the path.

After walking some distance and still reeling from the early wake up call, Joseph is walking alongside a narrow river with shallow banks. He gazes into the water as he plods along. The midmorning sunlight twinkles on the surface, only interrupted by lone branches or leaves floating by. His attention is interrupted by voices and as he looks up, he can see a bridge in front of him with a few chatting people perching on it. Once on the bridge, he looks over the side to continue watching the water. The multicolour show as the water clashes against the rocks is mesmerising. The haze creates a miniature rainbow; Joseph is struck with awe. He thinks with a smile, 'If God were to ever create a perfect moment, this must be one of them.' As he concentrates on the water, he slowly realises he can see silvery fish as big as the size of his hand. He plucks up the courage to catch a fish for lunch, so making his way down to the water, he takes off his backpack and jumps in with a splash. Hearing the commotion, the people who were on the bridge change sides to watch Joseph. The water is bitingly cold around his feet and legs. He bends over and crouches slightly and places his hands out like fans until they're almost touching the water, then waits.

Trying to concentrate, he targets a sizeable-looking fish and with a mental count of one... two... three... he strikes the water like a bald eagle striking at its meal. Missed! The people on the bridge giggle at the entertainment.

Joseph readies himself again; he pauses to concentrate. Then one-two-three, he whips into action. Lifting his hands up in the air, a fish wriggles between them. The people look on in amazement... only to witness Joseph drop the fish, lose his footing and fall backwards into the water, much to their giggling delight.

Picking himself up, he flicks the water from his dripping hands and arms to pad his wet clothing down. He quickly readies himself one last time. The onlookers are quick to fall quiet in anticipation of what may unfold. 'Come on, Joseph, you can do this!' he thinks. He steadies himself and takes a deep breath. Then one… two… three…! He plunges his hands in and quickly stands up. He lifts a fish above his head. His audience give him a cheer and applause. Smugly, he throws the fish high up onto the embankment and climbs out.

Picking everything up including his fish, he walks away with a swagger of confidence. After gathering some wood, he makes a small fire and cooks the fish in his new found pan and enjoys it with a great sense of satisfaction. With a full stomach, Joseph lays his back on the ground and reminisces about his swim, smiling. 'Overall, I'm not managing too badly. If only William could see me now…' Then he remembers the farmer's seething voice, the darkness of the barn and the sound of the warning shots reverberating through the open field. 'It's not like I'd ever have to tell him.'

Perhaps it was the aftertaste of the fish or too much time spent in the afternoon sunshine, but Joseph suddenly felt feverish, his good mood waning. His attention is drawn to the sky. He stares at the clouds directly above as they move and, using his imagination, he traces his finger in the air, outlining distorted images of animals, people and objects. It doesn't take long before he's fast asleep.

He wakes, sitting upright, with a start. Rubbing his face

half with shock, and partly to rub the sleep from his eyes, he surveys the area around him. The fire has burnt out to a small glow, his now dry socks and shoes sit between the embers and himself, and the heavy clouds have started to form, darkening the sky inch by inch towards the setting sun in the distance.

Conscious of the dwindling light, Joseph trudges along the beaten track through open fields, over stiles, passing through gates while watching the distant farmhouses to pass the time. The deep trodden path snakes its way along, sometimes alongside the river, crossing over at various bridges. Signs of civilisation break off piece by piece. First, the farmhouses shrivel away behind hills and trees. Herds of sheep and cows that graze freely behind lopsided fences slowly vanish until the only sign of life are crickets clicking merrily or the careful rustle of a fox in the growing vegetation.

Hours pass before Joseph notices the enclosure of trees building over him; a cruel trick for nature to be playing on him. Stopping, lending his focus to his senses, a rhythmic clip-clop echoes through the trees. Joseph walks faster and breaks into a run when someone on a horse approaches from behind. The sound of the horse becomes so close that Joseph stops, hoping the stranger will pass. Instead, he hears the click of a pistol which, when he carefully turns around he sees aimed at his temple.

With a deep gravelly voice, the masked stranger orders, "Hand over your bag."

Joseph slowly moves his hand around his back as if to take off his backpack but reaches for the handle of a dagger hidden in the waistband of his trousers. After a moment's thought, he continues to take off his satchel and holds it out in front of him at arm's length.

The rider reaches over and snatches the bag out of Joseph's tight grip.

The rider says, "Close your eyes and count to twenty."

Shaking with fear, Joseph closes his eyes tightly and, stuttering violently, begins to count. "O-one, t-two, th-three, f-four, f-five…"

The stranger laughs and speeds away on his horse.

Still shaking and counting, "E-eleven, t-twelve…" Joseph can hear the sound of the hooves gradually fading away before daring to open an eye. He stops counting and breathes a huge sigh of relief, collapses to his knees, cups his face with his hands and sobs at the terrifying ordeal. Thinking to himself, 'How stupid I am to go off by myself. I should have listened to William.' Disoriented, he pulls himself together, wipes his eyes, dusts his clothes down and continues his journey in a demoralised stumble.

The weather closes in and it starts to rain. As he walks along, the rain is falling heavier and heavier. With little light left, Joseph looks up and can just make out a small wooded area in the distance. Hoping for refuge, he hurries toward it. Luckily he finds a tree with a hollowed out base; he crawls in and it feels like a snug fit – roomy enough to move a little but tight enough to feel safe.

He has no sooner nodded off when he is rudely awoken by the howling wind and leaves rustling loudly above his head. He can feel the tree moving around and hear the creaking of the timber. Joseph wills himself to go back to sleep despite the heavy tapping on the wood caused by the hard hitting rain. Deep in slumber, he dreams about the cabin in the Wood, William, and his family. Then his dreams turn into nightmares, reliving the torture of being robbed at gun point...

"No! Please! No!"

The gun fires.

Breathless, a startled Joseph is woken in the middle of the night, panting and sweating through his clothes. The sound of barking in the distance piques his senses. He thinks to himself, 'Bloody hell! It must be a pack of wolves!'

The barks grow to a crescendo... a choir of howling.

'Lord help me!' Eyes widening and pupils dilating with fear, he clasps his hands together and starts to pray that they run past. The wolves are stealthy, deadly quiet as they roam nearby Joseph who silently prays... that is, until he can hear rapid sniffing. He gasps and slams a hand across his mouth to block any sound. His eyes are so wide with fear that they're almost popping out of his head as he holds his breath, not daring to make any subtle movement that could draw them near.

The vigorous sniffing intensifies, then there's a loud bark followed by a chorus of deep rumbling growls. The paws claw and scratch at the timber base. A wolf latches onto a piece of his hooded coat that is flapping in the gusts of wind. With deep long growls, the wolf pulls more ferociously at his coat.

With nothing to hold onto, Joseph is dragged out. The fabric shreds into fibres in their drooling jaws. He reaches for his long stick and starts to lash out and wave it around. He hits the wolf until it whimpers and lets go of his coat.

Joseph stumbles to his feet and starts to scream loudly, "AARG! AARG!" and shakes his stick around in an attempt to keep the wolves away. They prowl around in an organised pack, trying to gain the best vantage point.

Once in the perfect position to attack, one of the wolves suddenly darts past Joseph. He can feel the sudden shock of hot breath against his freezing fingers. The wolf rips the stick from his hand, leaving only a slither of drool. Seconds later, another leaps up from behind him and knocks Joseph to the ground. A third wolf lunges towards him, growling, with snarling teeth that are ready to bite, but Joseph swings a tightly clenched fist as fast and as hard as he can.

His fist slams into the wolf's snout and the creature flies into a heap on the floor, whimpering pathetically. Yet, another beast takes the previous wolf's place, creeping in readiness to pounce. Fatiguing and lacking an escape route, Joseph thinks, 'This is the end,' and holds his arm up across his face, wincing through a splay fingered hand. A fourth wolf slowly prowls towards his feet, all bared teeth and snarls. It drools, growling with every step.

Joseph's eyes widen in terror upon seeing the whites of its eyes glisten under the moonlight and feeling the wisps of vapour like white fire from every rhythmic pant. Its eyes are bloodshot, making it seem like a four legged demon. Then, the wolf lowers its limbs to the ground.

Joseph squeezes his eyes shut anticipating a tremendous pounce. Yet moments pass.

When he opens his eyes, the wolf flies not towards him but into the adjacent tree, knocked away by a flying log, too stunned by the impact to mewl.

A large shadowy figure looms over Joseph, waving a burning stick.

"YAAH! YAAH!" comes the familiar deep voice of William.

The wolves waste no time in scurrying away, whimpering and howling.

Joseph bawls into his hands with relief, scrambling towards his friend.

William comforts him with a hug. "Come on, let's get out of here before they come back," he says.

Picking themselves up while the rain pours down, they make their way to the next town.

CHAPTER 8

Arriving in the town completely soaked through to the skin, they agree to sacrifice a few coins for a bed and a hot dinner. The following morning, a shrieking cockerel wakes them up and the haze of day breaking fills the room, gold specks trickle around the air and settle into the quietness of the room.

"Look over there, Joseph," says William, pointing towards a thick wide tree. "That's an oak tree. Oak is harder than elm but elm has an interlocking grain that makes it much, much tougher than oak."

The memory evokes a smile. Although quiet and warm in bed, Joseph pictures the sun glinting off the variety of greens and textures, and the way William's younger eyes gleamed with warmth and kindness.

"What are you smiling about?" asks William.

"Oh, nothing," answers Joseph.

"Well, let's get up and dressed – then we'll be on our way," says William.

They no sooner set off walking when Joseph realises the town is far off in the distance behind them. Neither one of them speaks a word for the best part of an hour, before Joseph asks, "I'm glad you are here, but what made you follow me?"

William releases a shaky laugh. "I realised no money is

worth the peace of mind I get knowing you aren't mauled to death by wolves No, honestly, I felt bad seeing you go on your own. And, well, a little guilty. You're more important to me than the workshop. It'll be there when I get back," he shrugs.

Along their hike, they meet a section of river. Joseph spends the journey telling of his adventures, recounting to William the horrors and successes from the past three days. Being the first time venturing into the world together (a world beyond Hopewood), Joseph fails to notice how William grimaces through the re-enactment of the farmer and his shotgun. Nor does he pay attention to the glint in William's eyes when motioning the size of the fish he caught.

Lost in conversation, William points to a sign that reads 'London 20 miles'.

"I think when we get there that if we haven't found them after, let's say three days, we'll head back home. If that's agreeable with you?" asks William gently.

"We'll find them," grins Joseph.

Inside the bustling metropolis of the capital fills, Joseph's eyes bulge at the sheer scale of it all, and a feeling of trepidation creeps in again. Hopewood seems a world away. On the city streets, a river of people weave in and out of one another in a flurry of colour. Joseph fixes his eyes on to one thing, only to blink and find it vanishing as fast as it appeared.

The scene playing before them changes rapidly while

William's knuckles grip onto Joseph's arm, turning white. And the smell is not for the faint of heart: rotten food mixed with urine and a good helping of manure. There are pleasant ones, too, like the smell of beer, sugary treats and the odd waft of perfume from the well-dressed ladies and gentlemen as their carriages pass by.

William drags Joseph past a roasted-chestnut vendor. A plethora of people meander along the hectic street; with so many different people in an array of shape and colour and size, he notices how nobody seems to stare and gawk, even when he absentmindedly bumps past their shoulders. Arms and elbows prod into their backs and angry voices poke out in the sea of strangers, all in a mumbling inaudible blur.

Joseph's head whips back and forth when he feels William's grip disappear. 'In fact', he observes, 'nobody looks at *each other*. I could have three heads and barely a stitch on me and I still bet nobody would turn their head!'

They walk through the streets and, as Joseph tries to keep up with William's strides, Joseph almost has a lighter bounce in his hurried steps. The two of them reach a quieter part of the street, and are able to catch their breath when they sit down on the steps of a very grand ornate building and have a bite to eat.

William tries to make a plan of what to do next, but his attention is distracted by the noises coming from a nearby street market.

"I have an idea! Let's go along there," he says, pointing

towards the market. "We can get some more food and hopefully find a place to stay for the night," he adds.

After finishing their food, they head for the market. The sight is something from the stuff of dreams. The multicoloured fabrics are dazzling to the eye. The pair try to keep their wits about them and keep on track from all the distractions. William looks around and sees a sign hanging down outside a building which reads 'The White Hart Inn'.

"Joseph, if you wait outside, here, for a moment, I'll ask if they have any rooms," says William. Then, he removes his bag. "Can you keep this safe for me?" he asks while handing Joseph the bag. After a nod from Joseph, he disappears inside.

Joseph leisurely sits himself on the steps. He takes his bag off from over his head and places it in between his feet. He looks around at the market, at all of the traders shouting for attention. The hustle and the bustle of everyone buying and selling makes the scene look like organised chaos. He can hear so many different sounds, metal pans, rustling of jewellery, the chinking of coins all blended into a strange but pleasing buzz. Spices, meats, fruit and vegetables give the air an aroma, that if you were to close your eyes, it could transport you to another world: India, Mali, Turkey – places familiar from Zelda's prattling.

He scans the stalls and wares, resisting the temptation to run his fingers over all the trinkets on offer. As he looks more closely, he notices a heavily grained wooden box. Sitting on the steps, his stare is transfixed on the box and his heart sinks when he thinks about his old box. 'What happened to it?' The more he stares at it, the more he wants it. He slides his hand into his pocket and pulls out his pouch of coins. Cupping the pouch with his two hands, he is careful to open it and counts them. One… two… three…

He's interrupted by the Inn door opening and William's voice.

"I've got us a room for two nights. It wasn't cheap," he announces.

Joseph quickly closes his pouch of coins and places them back into his pocket.

William sits next to him on the steps. "We have two nights, so if we can't find them by the day after tomorrow, we'll have to go back to Hopewood. Yes?"

Joseph shrugs and then nods.

"Come on then, we best make a start. I'm thinking if we walk around the streets and look inside a few pubs, we can ask anyone if they know anything," he says as he pats Joseph's knee. "Let's go."

Quick to their feet and after wading through the market, they briskly walk up the street to commence their search.

Each person they see and approach, they ask, "Do you know an Esme and Richard Adams?" They ask person after person. A disgusted 'no' or a blank shake of the head is their constant reply.

While they're walking along, Joseph can hear the muffled din of music. It piques his interest; it's something he has never heard before and it seems to be coming from a building further along the street. As his eyes wander, seeking out the origin of sound, he momentarily forgets about the search all together. His feet blindly follow the sound, and with William in tow they're soon both standing outside a particularly rowdy pub… the music is so loud the building should be shaking. Joseph places his hand on the wall and the vibrations send a tingling sensation through the bones in his arm.

Joseph steps back slightly, looking to William who signals Joseph to join him at the doorway with a side nod of the head.

As Joseph approaches with hunched shoulders and a thudding heart, William pushes open the door and looks to his son. Noticing an involuntary shudder, William says to Joseph, "It'll be alright," with a toothy grin.

Stepping inside, they're surrounded by an ambience of merriment, locals singing, while others sit at tables playing card games. A smartly dressed and aged gentleman wearing a bowler hat plods merrily at a piano. Ladies dressed in can-can style dresses and feathers are dancing around the room encouraging others to have fun.

They try to ease their way around the room and ask everyone they squeeze past, which proves to be pointless: nobody seems to pay any attention to the enquiries made, not that the lively atmosphere would allow them to hear any reply regardless.

William taps Joseph on his shoulder and nods towards

the door. Joseph immediately understands and they both shuffle timidly towards their exit.

Back outside, the pair gasp the open air and continue up the street.

Joseph walks with his head bowed. Upon seeing an old beaten up can in the road, he kicks it with all his might and shouts, "We're never going to find them, are we?" The can narrowly misses William.

"I'm not sure," answers a tiring William. "But we only have a day to go. And we don't actually have a sound plan."

"I might," he pauses. "I might not go back," says Joseph, rubbing the palms of his hands together in frustration.

"What do you mean? You can't stay here! There's nowhere for you to stay," states William dryly.

"Why?" asks Joseph.

William takes a moment to gather his thoughts and says, "You don't know how bad this place can be. The city has very dark places. And not everyone will be nice or kind to you. This isn't Hopewood."

"If I can survive in the Wood, I'll be fine here," states Joseph.

"This is a different place with different people, and neither will care about you," is the response.

Joseph retreats by a step and clenches his fists. "You're making me angry."

After a heavy sigh, William throws his arm around Joseph and says reassuringly, "I don't want to make you angry, son. I want you to be safe. Come on, it'll be alright. We'll find them."

They move through the myriad of streets with a more unsettling awareness of how precarious their situation truly is. Some streets seem to never end but by turning one corner, it would seem to lead them into what seemed to be a maze of houses and buildings. Street by street and road by road, they check each public house and shop as they go.

William notices a sign along the road for another, more remote pub just as the daylight is starting to fade.

"No more," Joseph says. "We need to head back to the Inn now, William. My feet are tired."

As the hours they spend walking back pass, the futility of their mission sinks in for Joseph. It is early hours of the dark morning when they both collapse onto their beds in their cramped hotel room.

Both wake up to the loud noises out on the street, horse hooves and cart wheels rushing past, the morning's market traders setting out their stalls and raised voices of pedestrians passing by chattily. Waking up with a stretch, they both dress in what little space they have and after having breakfast, they head out to start their search again but this time in the opposite direction: person after person, street after street, business after business but to no avail. In the same fashion as the previous day, they find the further they go, the more run down the streets appear to be.

As the day progresses, Joseph becomes deeply demoralised and a sick feeling in his stomach crawls its way up to his chest, which only spurs his determination to continue the search more. Feeling the warm sun beating down on them, he wipes his brow and says, "Can we stop for a bite to eat?"

"Aye," replies William, "but we should be more careful with our money. We haven't got much left and we'll need some to get back home. There's an eatery along the street, let's go and sit in there and rest our legs."

Entering the dingy-looking tea room, the place is semi-full of unscrupulous-looking characters all huddling around their own tables having noisy conversations. An instant silence dampens the atmosphere, as though their entrance flips a switch among the drinkers; their demeanours turn murderous.

"Come in, gentlemen! Take a seat. I'll be over in a moment," says a haggard-looking woman, looking up from behind the counter with a rough husky voice.

And everyone returns to their own business.

As they squeeze past the unkempt customers, the pair observe how seemingly the underbelly of society are all there. Joseph can't help but feel a huge sense of dread as they sit on one of the few remaining tables.

Before they know it, the lady is standing at the end of the table.

"What'll it be?" she asks while holding a tea-towel in her clenched fist on her hip, as she uses her free wrist to wipe her nose.

"Can we get two kedgeree, please?" William orders. "And two beers, as well, please," he adds, taking out his pouch of money discreetly.

The exchanging of coinage catches the attention of the inhabitants on the adjacent table; they feign nonchalance, and suddenly turn around again when William smiles to them. The oblivious waitress exposes a grin showing only every other tooth, and retreats behind the counter.

After a few moments of awkward silence, Joseph mutters, "Do you think we'll ever find them?"

"I don't know, but we'll keep looking," William roughly whispers back.

Their dinner is served swiftly and as they tuck in, William glances around the room between mouthfuls of food. A shadowy vagrant lurks, observing the pair from the corner.

William eats at a faster pace.

Joseph senses that something is wrong and scans the room, observing the customers watching and whispering about them.

As the pair hastily finish their food, William wipes his chin with a napkin, stands and says in Joseph's ear, "I'm going to use the john and we'll be on our way."

Passing the dishevelled woman behind the counter, he disappears along a dark and narrow passage to the rear yard. Moments later, Joseph notices the light around him darken. He focuses his eyes onto the dregs of the plate in front of him, and not the crowd growing around the table. Joseph drops his spoon and pushes his plate away when a man sits in William's place.

"Boo!"

The surrounding crowd erupts into laughter. Joseph laughs along with them, trying to ignore the enormous ragged scar running across the stranger's face from temple to jaw. Beefy and gruff, the man has food stuck in the thick bristles of his ginger beard. Gold bands glisten off the thick pork sausage fingers folded together on the table.

"Mary, love!" he calls out in a heavy cockney accent. "Beers all around! Our new chum looks like a generous chap."

Joseph shares a little smile to appease the cheering crowd.

Shrugging his shoulders and wiping his nose with those grubby fingers, the man turns to Joseph. "Come on then, son. Let's have the bees and honey." Any trace of humour vanishes. "Give us your bees and honey!"

"But we didn't order any bees or honey," Joseph, blankly, innocently, chokes out.

An arm reaches from behind Joseph's field of vision, lifting him to his feet by the collar.

As Joseph struggles, kicking his feet in a panic, members of the crowd take a limb each.

Meanwhile, the ringleader remains seated, pan-faced, and sniffs grotesquely before simply saying, "You'll want to play nice with us, son. Liars aren't welcome round here."

The room turns deathly silent as Joseph gasps for air.

Between heavy breaths, he spits out, "Look! We only had kedgeree." Joseph cowers under the thug's raised fist when a familiar deep voice thunders from behind the men.

"Take your hands off him. Now." William slowly clenches his huge fists down by his sides in preparation.

The men all look in William's direction and say in unison, "Or what?"

The men hold a tighter grip onto a struggling Joseph while their leader slowly rises, doubling William's height and stature. In mocking Queen's English, he jibes, "And a-who do you think you are, you bleedin' pig."

"I'm his *dad*, you meater!" William dispenses two lightning fast heavy blows, sending the first two men flying over tables in opposite directions.

The leader throws a punch, aiming for William's face. Expertly dodging the stone fist, William throws his head against his opponent's. With eyes rolling and blood splattering, the ruffian slumps to his knees and face-plants the floor.

Ushering Joseph with his hand, Williams whispers, "Come on. Let's go."

As they quickly step over the incapacitated obstacles, they retreat and hurry down the road.

Once they turn the corner and pass a number of streets in silence, they pause. William places his hand on Joseph's shoulder. Tightly shrugging his shoulders and surrendering his hands, Joseph looks William in the eyes and says, "What happened? What did I do wrong?"

"They wanted your money." William stares blankly at him.

"But they kept asking for our bread and honey?"

"It's the way they talk around here, it's like a code," William explains gently.

"Well, how am I supposed to know that's what they wanted? I would have just given them it. You might be right: it *is* a bad place," Joseph sighs.

"And that's why I worry about you, Joseph. You shouldn't give in to bullies, and you can't just trust that everyone who seems nice is a friend. I thought you would know better." William's voice turns grave.

Joseph's face falls and, in a beat, William retorts, "So let's just be glad they all talk in riddles around here. Bees and honey... Sweet lord. Wait 'til we get home! You'll have Zelda in hysterics." William playfully grabs him in a headlock and ruffles his hair. "Don't worry your head over that, Joseph. We still have to find your parents, remember?"

Once again, the daylight quickly fades into evening darkness. With every boom of Big Ben, hour by hour, Joseph speeds his walking pace a little faster. London smog settles like a thick blanket on the cobble stones as they stalk the Thames and veer into the winding side streets, desperately asking every stranger that passes the same questions.

Joseph, worn out and defeated, sits on the steps of St Paul's half asleep.

William says, "It's time we got back, it's near on ten and

we're both dead on our feet. We need rest. It's going to be a long day tomorrow going back to Hopewood."

Joseph gives a big sigh. "Fine."

CHAPTER 9

With little to pack and little to say, Joseph and William spend the morning awkwardly checking over their room before leaving the hotel. While William converses with the hotel staff, Joseph sits on the steps of the entrance, pensively, watching the people at the market. Joseph looks around at the sellers, remembering the box. To his amazement, he sees that it is still sitting there under a striped canopy on a wooden stall. Glancing back to see William chatting animatedly with a young man in an apron, Joseph stands and wanders towards the centre of the market. Approaching the stall, the dazzling array of items are almost hypnotising. Some are made of silver, some with jewels and others with intricate carved decoration. There is glamorous jewellery hanging on the sides of the stall but after drinking in the display, he sees the highly polished wooden box with a gilded bronze horse raised in centre of the lid in the middle of the table.

Mumbling to himself, he says, "Uncanny. A little like the box I lost." Joseph points to the item. "How much is this?"

"To you… two silver coins!"

He very carefully takes out and hands over the coins. He quickly places the box in his bag, wrapping it in a piece of clothing. He hangs his bag over his shoulder and turns to seek out William when a loud and grating voice catches his attention.

"Alright then, Johnny, I'm off for my lunch. I'll be back in an hour and take over for the afternoon. Want anything getting while I'm…" The stranger's voice trails off as Joseph turns to face him, agape. The stranger drops the tray full of ornate artefacts in his hands.

Joseph's heart thumps and rattles against his rib cage. His throat clenches like the air is knocked out of him. For a single moment, the earth has stood still. For a single moment, Joseph is a small and afraid little boy again.

"YOU BLEEDIN' IDIOT, FREDERICK!" The stall owner moves to hold his assistant by the scruff of his neck, until Joseph pushes the red-faced, balding man out the way to tackle the stranger brother in a bear hug. For a single moment, he is looking up to his brother's face and that lost feeling has gone away. They hug so tightly it seems to squeeze the tears from Joseph's eyes and his smile stretches from ear to ear.

Frederick immediately places his hand on his shoulder. "You're here! You're really here!" he says with his hand covering his mouth in disbelief and a shocked look on his face.

George, the stall owner, looks back and forth between his clumsy assistant and the mess of ceramic shards on the floor, lost for words. "I'm taking you home to mother and father – they'll be beside themselves when they see you!"

Joseph pulls back slightly and says, "I need to wait here for William," just as William exits the hotel.

"William! Look! It's Frederick!" shouts Joseph, with a teary, bright smiling face, waving to get William's attention.

"Hello! Frederick!" William says, running over to the stand with a surprised grin. "It's great to see you. All big and grown up."

"The damages are coming out of your wages, Frederick!" blusters the stall owner.

"Oh sod off, you old cabbage. I'm taking the day off!" And the three men hurry out of the market, laughing and smiling the whole walk to their parent's house mere streets away. Once there, he asks the two to wait outside so he can spring the surprise to the family. Frederick saunters into the house, leaving the door wide open. He tries his hardest to contain his excitement and they hear him shout, "Guess who I've brought home?"

"Not another fancy lady. Who is she this time? A can-can dancer?" His father chuckles from behind a newspaper.

Joining in the joke, his mother's voice japes from the kitchen, "Don't tell me… it's another opera singer."

Then after a moment's wait, he shouts, "Come inside, you two!"

The whole house stops.

Daisy, screaming, instantly throws her arms around Joseph like her life depends on it and immediately cries tears of euphoric joy. Richard joins and embraces his arms around the two of them, too, shedding tears. Joseph sits between his mum and dad with William sitting opposite and Daisy can't stop staring at him as she surveys every inch of him and grips his hand like she's frightened to let go.

"I can't believe you are actually here! We sent word through the post but everything got sent back," she explains with tears welling in her eyes and her chin trembling.

"It doesn't matter now," says Joseph as his eyes well up, as though all the woes, trouble and time lost is irrelevant.

Richard wraps his arm around Joseph's back, reassuringly pats his shoulder and says, "I'm over the moon you've found us. Your mother and I haven't stopped thinking about you."

William sips at his cup of tea quietly. All four of Joseph's elder siblings pile in to the living room around the lit fire, distributing biscuits and small cakes between themselves, settling in to the excited conversations.

The hours pass by with everyone sharing stories to fill the gaps of time passed which carries through to the evening over a hearty meal of mince and dumplings.

Joseph surveys the whole table: his parents, his friend, his siblings. His loved ones. An inner sunshine glows from within and the feeling is unfamiliar. The darkness of his childhood and from his secluded life in the Wood, he muses, was worth it to feel this happy. 'I'm not going to spoil this happy time by thinking about all that. I am going to sit at a table surrounded by love and enjoy my evening, best day ever.'

Looking at his brothers and sisters all grown up seems,

to him, a little strange. Frederick, once thunderous and so much taller than a younger Joseph, has grown into a man shorter than Joseph's stature with rosy cheeks and a melodic laugh. His sisters, once shrill and secluded to themselves and always conspiring mischief, are almost unrecognisable with their warm glow.

They all continue to chat and sing into the early hours which heals the loss of Joseph's last fifteen birthdays missed.

Sensing the impromptu party drawing to an end as everyone starts to tire, Richard stands and says, "Our family has been through some difficult times, none more so than the thought of losing a son. However, with the help of great friends," he glances at William as everyone smiles towards him, "I believe that when life throws you a second chance, you should grab it with both hands. Now our family is together again, thanks to William, and there's nothing more important than that. With that in mind I'd like to propose a toast." He thrusts a glass aloft. "To family."

Everyone holds the glasses in the air. "To family!" they declare.

The next few days pass when William says to Joseph, "I really must return to Hopewood tomorrow. I'm assuming you want to stay?"

"Must you leave? We're all having such a good time. I don't want it to end."

"The workshop won't run itself, lad."

"And you wouldn't mind if I stay, would you?" The pair exchange a warm and tender hug. "I can't thank you enough. You truly are my best friend," he adds.

After they wave farewell to William, his siblings march Joseph out with a whole day planned to explore the city. Visiting the attractions and famous landmarks like the Zoo and London Bridge, Joseph is in awe of everything. After passing through Camden, they call into The Flask public house for refreshments.

They all gather around a table with drinks, chatting and joking. Joseph is enjoying a cold drink when he catches a glimpse of the barmaid. She has rosy cheeks, long blonde hair and a head scarf to hold it in place. He is transfixed by her beauty.

The conversation slowly settles to a lull and after a while, Joseph realises his brothers and sisters are watching him, too. He turns his attention back to the group and gives a sheepish grin. The chatting stirs again when Frederick orders more drinks. The barmaid distributes the tankards one by one and catches Joseph looking at her, blushing.

In between Frederick and Joseph, she collects the empties. Joseph passes one of the glasses over to her. It slips out of his grip and it smashes on the floor. The whole room erupts into cheering.

"Oh! I am so so sorry! I can pay for the damage!" Joseph gushes and moves to pick up the chunky shards when the barmaid puts her hand in the way.

"No, honestly, it happens all the time in here. You'd think

you'd never been inside a pub before." She crouches down, minding her skirts to clean up and accidentally bumps her head against his. Laughing and rubbing their foreheads, she helps Joseph up to stand and their eyes lock.

"This is Joseph," Frederick says after clearing his throat, and he nudges Joseph's shoulder with his.

"I should use a broom. Nobody move." She blushes awkwardly, rushing off, tiptoeing over the glass. When she returns, she fidgets with her hair obsessively and begins sweeping.

"I'm Rose." Her attention focuses on her sweeping but her eyes flick up momentarily to catch Joseph's awestruck gaze.

"Would you like some help, miss?" asks Frederick.

Giving a little cough, she replies as she breaks away her eye contact. "No, honestly. You're better off staying where you are. If someone gets cut, I'll hit the deck. Blood makes me faint."

Lost for words, Joseph's mouth dries and his pulse races. The best he can think to do is listen to his brother chatting away to the barmaid. Although he tries to join in the conversation, he trips over his words or loses his train of thought when he dares to look at her. Even when Rose senses him looking and returns the eye contact, his heart skips a beat and he looks down at his hands.

Rose retreats behind double doors with the shards in a pan and Frederick gently nudges his brother and says, "You idiot! Why aren't you talking to her?"

"You're doing such a good job of it," Joseph scowls.

"Come off it. She's just being nice because she's clearly hoping you'll say something to her." Frederick smiles knowingly at his other siblings.

"You really think so?" Joseph warms at the thought.

"And she's a bit like you. You like her, don't you?"

"Of course I do! She's perfect," Joseph says.

They finish their drinks and head for the door, Joseph meandering as slowly as he can. He purposefully makes sure he is the last out of the tavern and as he leaves, a petite hand on his upper arm stops him.

"It's Joseph, isn't it? I never forget a face so I know I've not seen you in here before. Will you be back in tomorrow?" she asks.

"I'm not sure. I'm not from around here. Why?" he says.

"Well, if you're not from around here, I can show you the sights. You could buy me lunch?" she suggests with a glowing smile.

"Yes, please, that sounds fun," he replies.

"Meet me here tomorrow around mid morning," she says.

With a fluttering stomach, Joseph leaves the pub with his siblings, barely grasping the conversations, jokes and teasing shared at his expense.

Leaning against the lamppost outside the public house, Joseph fidgets with the neckerchief itching at his neck, checking the pocket watch tucked into his waistcoat on loan from his father. Red faced, he scratches the back of his head.

Hair wispy and cheeks flushed, Rose bounds with a flurry of skirts up to Joseph and straightens his cap before grabbing his hand and leading him off on their tour. Chatting melodically between explanations, bits of social gossip and personal anecdotes, Joseph blushes like a lobster every time he makes contact with her deep sapphire eyes.

As the pair of them are walking along a high hedge-lined street, they arrive at an ornate pair of wrought iron gates left ajar. Once through, they find a large open grassy area that has large trees randomly planted like they've been sprinkled into place by a giant's hand. Joseph felt peaceful being surrounded by the grass and trees; it stirred memories of Hopewood.

"You look really nice," blurts out Joseph, feeling he should say something.

Pausing for a second, Rose giggles. "You're sweet. But my hair is a mess and I've been on the go since six this morning." Sensing an awkwardness in Joseph, she continues, "So if you're not from around here, where are you from?"

"Hopewood – it's a small town, a few days away," he answers.

"What do you do there?" she says.

"I work in a carpenter's workshop. I help to build and fix furniture," he replies. As they pass an oak tree, Joseph taps it with his hand. "I work with my dad."

"I thought you only just found your dad? From what you all were chatting about yesterday, I thought…"

"Yes, it's all a bit long and complicated. I suppose I have two dads. I'm just lucky that William also happens to be my best friend. We go into the local Wood for supplies, but each time we go it's like an adventure. The rustling of the leaves, the sound of the birds singing and the different smells are wonderful. Like they are in this field but better. More colourful. More rich. Well, they were when I lived in Hopewood. I suppose I live here now." Turning pensive, Joseph's voice trails off as his eyes fixate on a flock of birds flying overhead.

Rose grabs his hand, examines the palm and remarks with a smile, "You have strong working hands. They're nice and soft, too, but what are these little dark spots?"

"They're from the splinters I sometimes get. I have to get William to take them out for me. They don't half bloody hurt!" Joseph answers, laughing. "Have you always worked in the pub?"

"I've lived there my whole life. I think I got used to a busy and loud room with busy and loud people a long time ago – you have to have a big voice to work in the pub. And laugh. And not care about things much. But you're different... you're quiet. You don't hide anything, either. I like that," she says grinning, looking down at the ground and curling her hair behind an ear.

The more they talk, the more he finds her company irresistible and the more infatuated he becomes.

Upon reaching the other side of the park, Rose waves her arm in the air and says, "And welcome to Buckingham Palace."

Joseph stares in awe at the size of the grand building. Pristine soldiers guard the perimeter in smart red military outfits with huge fur headdresses and a rifles sloped from hand to shoulder. He lifts his eyes to see the multiple extra large windows. His gaze wanders farther up to find the Royal Standard flag flapping in the breeze, making it seem like a cherry on a cake.

"Someone very rich must live there!" says Joseph.

Rose quickly places her hand over her mouth as she lets out a big laugh and sarcastically states, "Yes. Only Queen Victoria."

Passing through a crowd of tourists to see the Palace from a different angle, Joseph tries to keep up with Rose who is barging her way boldly through the throng. "Her arms must really ache washing all those windows," says Joseph.

"It's one of the pleasures of having servants," answers Rose.

After spending a while looking around the palace, Rose sticks one hand in the air and whistles with the other. "Come on, Joseph. We'll catch a ride in a cab."

A horse drawn single-wheeled carriage pulls up to the curb.

"The Tower of London, please," says Rose, before climbing in and pulling Joseph up by the elbows quickly as the cab sets off. He looks out of the window and watches the people going about their business, most of whom are smartly attired men with walking canes and top hats, and ladies in glorious flowing dresses that carry delicately laced sun parasols.

As the carriage turns left, Joseph's eyes are drawn to a huge square building. His gaze follows the intricately carved stone and windows upwards, his mouth wide open in awe as his eyes look over the large domineering faces like a giant sized grandfather clock pointing at the heavens. He sits himself back into his seat, not wanting to ignore Rose. Accidentally, he places his hand on hers and for a few moments their fingers intertwine before she pulls away to let him sit more comfortably.

"This is all amazing!" says Joseph, beaming with a big smile. They lock eyes and hold each other's gaze as he slowly reaches for her hand again. Feeling lost for what feels like a brief second but long enough to make each other's hearts flutter, they both begin to lean forward for a kiss.

Suddenly, Joseph's nose smacks into Rose's forehead when the cab jolts to a stop. Bent over cradling his nose in agony, Rose bursts out laughing, holding on to his shoulder.

She covers her mouth to suppress her giggles and places her soft hand on his head to help ease the pain. "Let me see... no blood. You might bruise though, you poor thing."

"Get a wriggle on you two!" the cab driver bellows from the front of the carriage.

Joseph gathers himself together and as he lifts his

head, he is taken aback by the sheer scale of the Tower of London. The Yeomanry Guards are dressed in their red, black and gold military uniforms patrolling the area.

"Should we have some lunch down by the river?" suggests Rose. "We can buy something from a street seller."

Joseph nods in agreement.

They make their way to the river bank. As they approach the food sellers, Joseph's attention is stolen by the scene in front of him.

"That's a *big* bridge!" he blurts out, which makes Rose laugh as she places the food into her bag.

"We can walk across it if it really makes you that happy?" asks Rose.

"Yes, please," replies Joseph with a boyish look of excitement on his face. They make their way up to the busy road that leads round to the bridge. The pair walk along and wind through the heavily congested city street. The noises from the horse drawn buses and carriages along with the street sellers voicing their goods, newspapers, food and even flowers of all the colours you could imagine, make it difficult for Joseph to concentrate on where he places his feet. Luckily for him, Rose has a tight hold of his hand and pulls him along. After a short walk, they find themselves overlooking the flowing Thames many metres below.

Rose looks up and points to a sign that reads: *'Tower Bridge'*. Everywhere that Joseph looks seems amazing to him. A bascule and suspension structure with two square towers joined by two upper level walkways (and the roadway on the bottom) lifts up in half for ships to pass through. Loitering around the centre of the path, Rose spots a paddle steamer approaching the gap underneath. She grabs Joseph's jacket and pulls him closer to the railing.

"Watch this," says Rose. "As the boat passes under, the chimney blows hot air up and it feels funny on my face."

The paddle steamer nears the bridge, the noise of the engine and the paddles hitting the water seeming to hum in harmony. The chimney draws closer and closer.

"Ready? Three... two... one..." shouts Rose.

The hot air makes the skin on their faces flutter by itself and takes their breath away. Once the moment passes, they turn around and slump to the ground and look at each other and laugh like children. Rose reaches into her bag and hands out the wrapped food to Joseph.

"Pork pie?" asks Rose.

They both sit and eat their lunch, looking out over the east end of London. Momentarily, a coincidental break in traffic and pedestrians crossing, makes the city seem the perfect picture, almost idyllic, to the young couple. Despite the light rain, nothing can dampen their spirits or their feelings for each other.

Enjoying the pies and admiring the scenery, Joseph says, "Thank you for today."

"You're welcome," she replies before giggling.

They stroll back to the public house. Joseph escorts her back to make sure she arrives safely.

Standing on the doorstep, Rose says, "And thank you for a wonderful day. I really enjoy your company." She leans forward, places her hand on his chest and gives Joseph a quick peck on his cheek.

He catches a hint of her sweet perfume. She pulls her head back to momentarily look into his eyes and Joseph kisses her tenderly. He feels his knees weaken and it seems to take all his strength to stay standing. When they say the last of their goodbyes and Rose disappears inside, Joseph heads down the street in a haze of love with the biggest smile on his face and feeling deeply invincible. He punches the air and shouts out, "The greatest day ever."

CHAPTER 10

One year later

"We all chipped in together!"

"Do you like it? It's the poshest one they had in the shop!"

"And we know you don't have one, so we thought…" Frederick trails off, and his siblings all hush, watching their brother's reaction like hawks.

The tissue of the unwrapped box on the kitchen table rustles as Joseph gently runs his fingers around the brim of the top hat. The black felt fur, delicate and immaculate, glints a little against the morning sunshine.

"We want our brother to look his best on his big day!" Frederick broke the tension, laughing.

"Well, try it on!" says his mother, holding a mug of tea and observing her children from the corner of the room.

Everybody stares intently, holding their breath, as Joseph lifts the top hat from out of the gift box and places it on his head with a great sense of pride. A perfect fit.

"It'll make me look posh with my suit on," Joseph jokes.

The room erupts into relief, laughing and gushing, and fetching mirrors, and fetching the suit, and fussing over Joseph's hair. A barely audible knock from the front door goes unnoticed by the majority of the household when Daisy slips away from the frenzy, throws the door open absentmindedly and finds William standing there.

"Oh!" William and Daisy stare at each other for a moment. "Well, come in! Don't just stand there, you silly goose!"

With an awkward laugh, William steps over the threshold.

Joseph in his top hat, work clothes and socks pokes his head in to the hallway and, upon seeing William, rugby tackles him in a massive hug.

Ushering everyone back into the kitchen, Daisy shuts the front door, hangs back behind the group and sighs deeply. Sitting at the table with a plate of cake and custard, William between bites asks, "So, why did you need me to bring my suit then? The way you hugged me, I nearly thought someone had died."

"Do you remember Rose from my letters?" asks Joseph, blushing.

William nods.

"Well, a while back I went and asked her to marry me and I badly wanted to tell you but I thought a surprise would be better and I've spoken to Father and if you agree..." He pauses for a moment. "Will you be my best man?"

William's eyes open wide as the look of sheer delight beams from his face. Jumping up out of his chair, he exclaims, "I'll be honoured!"

After they hug, William reaches for his glass and raises

it up in the air. "A toast! To Joseph, a man for anyone to be proud of," he announces and takes a drink. Settling back down again, William says, "Rose is a very lucky lady."

"I think I'm the lucky one, William. Her family run a public house in Hampstead, so we're having a big party there afterwards," replies Joseph proudly.

"It's a good job I brought my suit," laughs William.

Zelda, Victoria, Lisa, Fiona, Thomas and Spencer sit in a row towards the front of the church with their parents, pulling faces at Joseph, who is standing, shaking slightly, by the alter. Lavish silk bows with beautiful multicoloured flowers are interwoven and are draped on the ends of each pew. Zelda's Mum catches Zelda mid face-pulling and smacks her knee when the church organ bellows through the church, the wedding guests hush suddenly, and Joseph jumps out of his skin. A young flower girl wobbles down the aisle, crushing white rose petals along the floor, and this elicits cooing and 'awww-ing' from the guests. At the altar, a display of matching colourful flowers have a vibrant impact against the drab grey stone walls.

Joseph, who is in his perfectly fitted morning suit, is taking deep breaths, fixing his eyes to the vibrant colours; nothing can wipe the smile from his face – but he constantly rubs his thumb across his palm as the odd bead of perspiration appears on his forehead.

The doors at the back of the hall fling open and Rose appears.

Joseph erupts into tears.

Giggling at him, Rose walks slowly in a full length silk dress with lace trim and intricate embroidered detail. When Rose joins Joseph at the altar, William hands his son a tissue and steps back to join the rest of the family on the front pew.

The priest begins the service – "Dearly beloved, we are gathered here today…"– while the two of them make endearing glances at each another with nervous smiles.

They both say their vows and exchange rings, then the priest says, "You may kiss your bride."

Joseph gently lifts the fragile veil up and over Rose's myrtle leafed tiara, embossed with fine wire leaves of sterling silver and blue inset sapphires. Sensing his shyness and hesitation as he leans over to peck her on the cheek, Rose pulls Joseph in for a passionate kiss. Rose's family hoot and holler and the congregation all laugh.

Wiping Joseph's tears away, she pulls back to look into his eyes and says, "There we are, then. Wasn't so bad, surely?"

The priest announces, "Ladies and Gentlemen, Mr and Mrs Adams."

The whole congregation cheer and applaud loudly with barely a dry eye in the house. The newlyweds saunter along the white rose petals, like they're walking on cloud nine, while the guests smile at them as they make their way out of the church. Outside, the bride and groom are bombarded with rice and lots and lots of well wishers congratulating them on their wonderful occasion before they both climb into a beautiful white horse drawn carriage decorated with flowers. Holding hands, they travel along the road, waving back at cheering strangers and stealing kisses from each other.

Arriving at the public house, Joseph exits the carriage, and offers a gentleman's hand to help Rose down. A huge rapturous applause greets the couple the second they walk through the doors. They're both taken aback by the highly decorated public house, streamers on the walls and across the lights, tablecloths covering the tables and signs along the bar reading, 'Just Married' and 'Congratulations'.

Each of them gratefully receives a glass of champagne and the celebrating continues into the early hours.

The next morning, Joseph wakes up next to his bride and gives her a loving kiss on her forehead as she sleeps. He looks up at the ceiling and thinks to himself, 'I'm not sure if this is what they call living happily ever after, I just know I've never been this happy. The greatest day ever.' He turns back round to watch Rose's peaceful face, a little drool sticking a piece of hair to her face. He tucks the strand back behind her ear, kisses her forehead gently and drifts back to sleep.

In the months after the wedding, Joseph and Rose start their married life above Rose's family pub, saving their pennies away from the barmaid work and Joseph's labour in the cellar. Towards the end of the following year, Joseph establishes his own informal carpentry enterprise, lugging casks of ale by day and fixing the neighbour's rickety chairs by night. By Christmas, Joseph is the local carpenter. By spring, the cellar is more workshop than ale storage. Rose often assists as Joseph reminisces about Hopewood, sanding down chair legs and sharing stories of his life in the Wood or the workshop with William, while Rose varnishes the finished pieces.

And by summer, the couple are well-established in their married and working life. The monotony of breakfast, pub hours, carpentry hours and then sleep suit them both well, making the honeymoon phase last.

A letter drops through the letter box with Zelda's familiar handwriting on it. Picking it up off the mat, Rose heads straight to the cellar.

Joseph catches a glimpse of Rose as she appears on the stairs holding a letter with a grin on her face. He excitedly abandons his tools and opens the letter like it's a present with a glint of delight in his eyes.

Dear Joseph,

I hope this letter finds you well! How is Rose? I still think of the wedding – it was such a beautiful day. I have been helping Mother with some baking, however she was not best pleased when I accidentally sneezed into the bowl of flour and both of our faces covered white. We laughed until our sides ached.

Miss Muggleton isn't very happy with the six of us, either. We were playing with a ball on the grassed area. Spencer threw the ball over Fiona, Victoria and myself… well, it was intended for Thomas to catch it, butter fingers that he is. Can you imagine what happened? Silly Thomas only dropped it and splashed the ball into the biggest, filthiest puddle and sprayed Miss Muggleton's dress with dirt spots. Her face was a picture! We honestly tried not to laugh but it was too funny. She was so furious with us all that we had to stand at the back of the class with our noses touching the wall. It was so funny we all spent an hour giggling uncontrollably. Just when I could calm myself down, Victoria or Thomas would set us all off again. Eventually, we became a bad influence because everyone else in the classroom started laughing, too! Miss Muggleton sent us all one to our parents shortly after, which stopped us giggling. Spencer's father looked absolutely furious when he saw the six of us walking home. I explained to Dad what had happened, though, and would you believe he was laughing with me as well? Good old Dad.

Father and I have begun another taxidermy project: a fox. It's fascinating! As we are working, sometimes, when I stare into the fox's eyes – it's almost as if I could see, just for a moment his cunning old personality.

I cannot be sure if William has been in touch with you about his accident in the Wood. I think some days he really struggles with his broken leg, poor William. My father has helped as best as he can – it's wrapped in bandages and splints on either side. Will you be coming to see him? He misses you terribly but he tries not to show it.

We all miss you and hope to see Rose and yourself again soon.

Your dear friend,

Zelda.

Joseph finds an empty barrel to sit on. As he slumps down, he stares into space and a frown spreads across his forehead. Sensing his distress, Rose approaches his side and places her hand on his shoulder to give him support.

"What's wrong?" she asks.

"William's had an accident and he's broken his leg. Zelda says he's struggling to manage," he explains.

"Oh no!" remarks Rose as she places her hand to her lips to try and hide the shock.

"I have to see him – he needs help. I'll finish this job and get things packed. I'm leaving for Hopewood tonight," he murmurs.

"No, you're not."

Joseph looks at her sharply and a smile blossoms on her face.

"God, I love you, Joseph, but your idea of packing is so messy it sends me loopy. Finish the job while I do the packing for you." Rose turns her back before Joseph catches her arm.

He places his finger under her chin and lifts her head, laying a light kiss on her forehead.

They gaze into each other's eyes a moment when he asks, "Would you come with me to Hopewood? We'll get to meet everyone again. I'll show you Hopewood and the Wood. We'll only be away for a short time – a week or two at the most. We've never been away from each other before and I…"

Her fingers brush his lips. "Say no more. You can't cope without me. We set off at lunchtime."

Joseph and Rose are sitting in the pub waiting to leave when Joseph asks, "How much longer do you think your father will be? I wonder what's causing the hold up – we really need to set off. It's a few days walk ahead!"

"My father said not to leave until he returns," replies Rose anxiously. She no sooner finishes speaking when the door flies open with her father bursting in. Huffing and puffing out of breath, his body leans against the door and the clippety-clop sound of hooves and snorts from horses can be heard from the street.

"Come out here, you two," says her father, nudging his head in the direction towards the door.

With curious looks on their faces, they immediately jump from their seats and grab each other's hand to head outside, passing her father in the doorway. Facing a stagecoach pulled by four majestic horses – beautiful and perfectly groomed, with thorough braces lined with leather and finished with brass fittings – leaves the couple speechless. They turn to each other, grinning, with their hands locked together.

The pair glance around to see Rose's father who is leaning on his shoulder against the lamppost, arms folded and smiling at their reaction.

Rose lunges forward, throwing her arms around him. "Thank you," screeches Rose as a happy tear rolls down her cheek.

"I wanted to make sure you arrive in Hopewood quickly and safely. Should shed days off of the travel time at least," he says.

"Thank you so much, sir," says Joseph, shaking his hand vigorously.

Rose's father pushes his hand away and pulls him into an embrace. Rose steps inside the pub posthaste and reappears with their luggage. After loading it all onto the stagecoach, Joseph opens the door to the carriage. He stands by the door proudly and almost to attention with anticipation, helping Rose into the carriage. She is shaking with excitement as he climbs inside, after her.

The coachman shouts "Yah!" The whip cracks and the carriage rattles forwards on the cobblestone path.

"Goodbye, Father," Rose shouts from the window, while waving her handkerchief.

Her father watches proudly as the wagon trundles along until out of sight.

CHAPTER 11

Hours of travelling pass by. Joseph gazes out of the window at the scenery, then as the landscape becomes more and more recognisable, he positions himself close to the door and peers out of the window to see the familiar outline of buildings in the distance. He slides back into his seat and takes a deep breath to calm the sudden bout of butterflies in his stomach.

Rose reaches out and places her hand on his knee for reassurance. "Are you feeling alright?"

He can only nod to answer, sitting upright, stoic and looking straight down while rubbing the palms of his hands together. He looks up and the pair lock eyes, which makes him smile. Rose returns a smile before Joseph turns his attention to familiar voices on the roadside. He sticks his head out to see Zelda, Fiona and Lisa playing hopscotch along the street.

Zelda catches a glimpse of the carriage, then points and shouts, "Look! It's Joseph!" The girls attempt to run to catch up with the horses when it stops abruptly. With sharp reflexes like the three musketeers and with the prowess of the Spanish Inquisition, the girls descend upon the doors ready to interrogate Joseph and Rose.

"What a great surprise! Zelda, you didn't say they were coming!" says Fiona.

"Are you back for good?" asks Lisa.

"It's great to see you again, Rose," gushes Zelda.

After all the hugging and once their excitement settles, Joseph says with a tired grin, "Hello, ratbags! We're exhausted from the long trip. Let's chat another time, eh? Pop over for tea sometime tomorrow. We need to see William."

Like a chorus, they all say in unison, "Yes! Of course."

The three of them joyfully bounce off in the direction of the common, while Joseph lugs the heavy suitcases to William's front door. Rose is looking in every direction to make sense of her new surroundings.

She takes a deep breath and says, "The air smells so clean and fresh…" Then, she tilts her head to one side. "With a hint of horse poo," she continues with a giggle.

William, unkempt and tired, peeks his head from behind the door and immediately displays the biggest smile, his eyes glowing with the instant realisation that Joseph and Rose are stood on his doorstep. With a stumble of his walking stick and a tear welling in his eye, William throws his arms around Joseph and hugs him tightly.

Once inside and settled, they all sit around the table with cups of tea and a light meal, and are soon sharing anecdotal stories. As the night draws on, the air is filled with laughter. Yawning, Rose heads off to bed leaving the two men chatting.

William readjusts his broken leg into a comfortable

position and places it on a chair. "Keeping it level helps to curb the pain," says William with a grimace.

"What happened? I've never known you to get hurt in the Wood," asks Joseph.

"Quite stupid, really," he says smiling. "I chose to fell a tree – a nice elm, too. I looked around as normal and started chopping the base. It took quite some time, as well. I'll be honest, I don't think it wanted to go without a fight," he continues while waving his arms around pretending to wield an axe. "By the time I'd gotten to the point of no return, my arms started to feel like lead weights. And then as it fell, one of the branches caught a log laid in the bracken. THWACK! Long story short, I didn't get out of the way in time. I think the tree tried to get me back," he laughs, wincing and bracing his head against the high back chair to alleviate the pain.

After laughing with William and a momentary pause, Joseph says, "We're staying for a couple of weeks to help you get back on your feet."

William gives a thankful smile while nodding and says, "It's getting late. Can you help me upstairs?"

Joseph helps him up to his room and then goes to bed.

Joseph is awoken in the early hours when Rose slips back into bed, eyes watery and forehead clammy. Propping himself up a little in bed, he turns to her and asks, "Are you feeling alright, love?"

"I think the change in water has sent me bad. The travelling won't have helped. Past couple of mornings

I've felt sick but I didn't want to wake you. It's not to worry, though. Now that we're here, the clean air will do me some good," she replies.

Joseph says, "Maybe it's the change of food, too? I know William's not the best cook."

"Yes, that's what I thought – probably bad meat when we've stopped off," she answers.

"Well, try and rest," he says.

He cuddles her as they fall back to sleep. Into the day, they potter around William's house, washing pots, making cups of tea, fluffing pillows and refilling hot coals into the bedpan. After tucking into a hearty dinner, William notices Rose has eaten only a bite or two and looks a little pale.

"Joseph, why don't you take Rose out for a walk? Show her the town square. Take her to the Wood, maybe? I'll be fine as I am and I think you've both been cooped up in here long enough. I have Mrs Harris next door if I need anything," William urges.

Rose suppresses a belch and nods at Joseph.

As they step out onto the street, the cool afternoon breeze immediately blows the cobwebs away and they take a slow walk along the high street. They both enjoy looking in the different shop windows and Joseph is keen to point out the bronze statue in the main square. He begins to explain the history behind the military figure and how the General was the founder of the town.

Rose interrupts him. "I've never seen you like this before."

"Like what?"

"This relaxed, this confident – I love it. It's a completely new side to you."

Joseph blushes lobster red.

"Oh, don't be embarrassed. I'm sorry, Joseph," she giggles. "I want to hear more about Hopewood. I promise I won't interrupt again. You were saying about…"

As they move on, Rose smells something wonderful. She looks around to see a baker's shop and as they approach it, the smell intensifies. They both look in the window to see a broad selection of different sized breads.

"We can get one on the way back if you want to?" Joseph suggests to her.

"Oooh, yes please," she replies.

Just as they were about to head off towards the Wood, they bump into Robert and Esme.

After exchanging merry pleasantries, Robert asks, "How would the two of you like to come over for dinner this evening? And please extend the invitation to William."

After Joseph glances at Rose, who responds with an encouraging, timid nod, he answers, "We'd love to."

"Thank you so much for the invitation," Rose beams.

Heading towards the Wood, Rose feels a little giddy, receiving their first invitation in town as a couple. Walking along, she holds Joseph's arm in a manner they normally would, except she holds his arm a little tighter, and her rosy cheeks bloom brighter.

When they reach the common Joseph holds his arm out in front and says hesitantly with a shaky voice, "This

is the Wood – it's where I lived for a while. My home."
As he stares blankly, Rose places her arm around him and
soothingly rubs his back.

"So you built a log cabin in the middle of *there*?" asks
Rose.

"I did," he answers. "Would you like to go and see
what's left of it?"

"Really? I'd love to," she replies.

They head into the Wood and as Joseph tries to clear
a way the best he can, he watches Rose like a hawk,
helping her over logs and obstacles, gripping her hand
tightly. Rose can feel a breeze blowing through the trees,
causing the branches to rustle loudly. Leaves whipping
up from the bracken-laden floor swirl around in mid
air like they're dancing. The sun's glow creates a golden
shimmer.

Rose feels like she's in a fairy tale. She stops and, not
wanting to miss a precious, magical moment, she quickly
grabs Joseph's hand. Then pulling him towards her, she
spins around to kiss him tenderly. When they eventually
open their eyes and gaze at one other's, she says, "I love
you."

"I love you, too," replies Joseph.

They wade through the Wood and the afternoon haze
fades the deeper they go. After a while, a pile of mangled
logs appears before them. The closer they approach the
wreckage, the more that the full extent of the damage
is evident. What was once Joseph's fantastical domicile,

entirely built by hand, now sits strewn in pieces like a jigsaw begging to be pieced back together. The roof, partially collapsed, points in all directions. Cordage hangs in coils from the corners and various logs have black burnt patches on them. Joseph walks slowly around, surveying everything. Rose can only stand there, her mouth wide open with shock. As Joseph approaches what was the front of the cabin, he notices the bottles have all fallen out of the window frame allowing him to see inside.

"Hey, Rose! Come around here. You can see inside," Joseph shouts. As she approaches the same window, she leans on the fragile windowsill to get a better view. Unable to wipe the shocked look off her face, she can make out the burnt remains of a bed and a table that is flipped on its side.

"What's that, there? It looks pretty," she asks, pointing to a wooden box on the floor of the cabin.

Joseph looks in the direction and his eyes can't believe it…

"That's mine! It's my wooden box!" he exclaims. Grabbing the nearest log to hand, he pivots around the cabin and levers the collapsing weight upwards to gain access but the logs are too heavy and he can only partially lift them. Placing the weight back down, he rubs his sore hands down the sides of his legs to discard the bits of bark and vegetation.

"Damn it!" he shouts. "It's too high! I can't get a good enough grip to pull it down."

Rose wanders curiously towards his position and looks at the area he is trying to access.

"Let's try it again. If we do it together, it might work," she suggests.

They both ready themselves and give an indicative nod. Joseph pushes down with all his might. Once the lever reaches down to waist height, Rose can clearly see the box and seizes her opportunity.

"Wait here…"

"What? Rose?"

"I've got it! Don't move a muscle!"

"Rose, I'll crush you!"

"It's alright. I trust you." Rose gives a little chuckle. She lunges towards the cabin's interior, steps between logs and crouches down to drag the box out.

"Rose, I'm going to slip! It's not worth it…" Red-faced and huffing, Joseph's muscles wobble and his knuckles turn white. Mustering all of his strength, he clenches his eyes shut and utters a small prayer. "Rose, I'm sorry. I'm so sorry." The sweat from his palms loosens his grip of the log. Eyes tight shut, his grasp slips entirely. "Shit! Oh my god, Rose! No!"

When the weight smashes to the ground, Joseph catches a glimpse of Rose crawling out adeptly from a tight space with the box under her arm. Pain instantly shoots through Joseph's face. An uppercut to his jaw from the recoiling lever sends him flying off his feet and onto his back with a thump.

Rose crouches next to him, stroking his face and still holding the box. "Are you alright?" she asks while trying not to giggle. "That was a bit of a nasty bump."

Scowling, he pushes her hand away. Between coughs, he chokes out, "How are you not dead? You're crazy."

Rolling her eyes, Rose helps him to sit upright. "Call me crazy as much as you like, I think I did a rather good job." A hint of a smile creeps on her face.

"It's not funny, Rose!"

And Rose bursts into a fit of hysterical laughter.

Wiping her streaming eyes, she says, "Here's your box."

Joseph pulls her into a tight hug and, wavering, says, "Thank you for my box. But don't scare me like that."

"And don't call me crazy - I really don't like that. Besides, I said I trust you. I am alive. And you have your box. You're welcome." She pecks his cheek sweetly.

"I'm sorry." He pecks her forehead in a returning gesture. "William might be right about the trees. I can't believe the box wasn't destroyed," he mutters. He slowly lifts the lid, with one arm still wrapped around Rose who readjusts to sit on his lap, to find all of the carved wooden figures and animals in immaculate condition. His shoulders shudder as tears roll down his cheeks. Rose simply holds him a little closer while he gently cries.

Once the tears ebb, Rose helps him up to his feet. He can't stop stroking the box. Sniffling, he looks at Rose and says, "Don't do anything like that again. Promise?"

"Yes, I promise," she sighs half-heartedly.

Holding her chin softly, he gazes into her eyes, "I thought I hurt you. Badly. But thank you so so much." Then he gives her a huge hug.

"Let's get back before the trees try to attack us again," says Rose jokingly.

CHAPTER 12

Back at William's house, they go inside to find William sitting at the table just finishing lunch.

"Hey, guess what I found," says Joseph.

"What?" replies William.

"My box," says Joseph, placing it on the table.

William can't believe his eyes and immediately starts to examine it.

"My goodness, I can't believe how it is miraculously still intact," he says.

"We are all invited to Robert and Esme's house for dinner. We bumped into them outside the baker's," says Joseph.

"Unfortunately, I can't go. But you two should! I'd feel uncomfortable in this predicament and I want to finish some jobs," replies William.

Later that day, a neatly dressed Joseph and Rose visit the Williams' home for dinner and are sharing funny stories. Rose mentions in passing how the change in water and diet is causing her to be a little poorly. Robert offers to help and suggests an examination to help put her mind at rest.

After a while, Robert emerges from his office and tells Joseph that Rose wishes to speak to him. He strolls in and

Rose takes a hold of Joseph's hand as he sits down and looks deep into his eyes. Her face is solemn.

"What's wrong?" he asks.

Rose smiles with tears in her eyes and says, "We are going to have a baby."

His mouth drops open and his eyes widen. "You mean?" he says, looking in her eyes. "You mean?" he repeats, looking at her stomach.

Rose nods as tears of joy run down her face.

Joseph throws his arms around her and they both hug and cry with happiness.

Moments later, Joseph and Rose emerge from the room and share the good news. "We're going to have a baby," says Joseph to everyone's delight.

While William is working in his workshop, he uses his crutches the best he can to move around. He hangs a lit oil lamp on a thick flat nail protruding from a beam. Grabbing the sweeping brush in hand, he starts to sweep and clumsily bangs his broken limb on the bench leg. Thrown off balance, William is sent spinning. His crutch is thrusted through the air, colliding with the oil lamp, which is sent crashing in the corner. A small fireball crawls up the side of the workshop. Feeding off the oil, sawdust and kindling, the fire climbs the walls and licks the thicker beams. William does his best to climb to his feet but each time is hindered by his broken leg. The flames rapidly spread through the area, burning everything in their path.

He quickly takes off his shirt and ties it to a stick he finds laying around and creates a fire beater. Initially, it seems to work as he hits the flames that are feeding off the saw dust. Then as he attempts the bigger fire, it seems to only fan the flames even more.

The fire is lapping at the ceiling like the Devil's tongue and a blanket of thick black smoke engulfs the rafters in the roof. The fire manages to burn through some rope that is holding a rack for tools and storing various pieces of wood and sends them raining down with a thunderous crash. The heavy rack swings out of control and as it goes to and fro, the weight causes the other rope to snap, sending it hurtling into William, knocking him out.

Joseph and Rose throw on their coats and exchange goodbyes with Robert, Esme and Zelda when they all hear loud shouts coming from the usually quiet street.

As they make their way towards the front door, the shouts and screams are louder. They all clearly hear someone shout, "FIRE! FIRE! At the carpenter's workshop!"

All five of them rush out into the street and look towards the workshop to see smoke bellowing out of the large doors and a strong orange glow.

"William!" shouts Joseph, heading towards the fire, quickly followed by the others.

As they approach, they join a crowd of people who are gawping and unsure of what to do. Robert is quick to organise a chain of people to supply buckets of water to throw at the fire.

Joseph pulls open one of the large doors and is immediately engulfed as a big rush of flames burst out.

Holding their hands in front of their faces to help them see through the flames, Robert points and shouts, "I can see William."

Robert takes off his shirt and tells Joseph to do the same. "Tie the shirt around your face to cover your mouth and nose to help stop the smoke," he instructs.

The pair rush through the doorway with their arms open for protection. The heat is incredible and energy sapping. They grab William's. Joseph hooks his arms and Robert grabs his legs. Being mindful of his broken leg, he crosses the leg over the other for support. As they stumble out, they carefully place William on the ground and collapse from exhaustion, coughing deeply from the thick black smoke. Their bodies are hot and sweating with smoke and steam rising from their shoulders.

The crowd gathers around them, cheering at their heroism, but Robert is fast to help William. "I can feel a heartbeat, but he needs a bed to rest in," says Robert.

While the crowd dealt with the fire, Robert and Joseph carry William next door to his bed with Esme and Rose's assistance. He lays unconscious in his tattered and singed clothes with a dirty face, his breathing shallow. "It's going to be a long night for him. With the thick smoke and heat damage, let's hope he has the strength to pull through," says Robert.

Rose glances at the clock… one o'clock. Feeling exhausted, she climbs the stairs to bed.

Joseph stays seated beside William's bed, holding his hand in the hope of detecting movement.

Joseph talks gently hoping it will provide comfort. "I remember you would let me help you, when no one else would even look at me. I remember feeling so lucky to have those carved figures and that beautiful box you made me… I will keep it forever." Joseph sobs and grips William's hand a little tighter. "I'll never forget that Saturday morning I helped you cut up the tree – I felt so big to be given that chance. You *have* to pull through this. You are… you are my best friend; you are my dad."

Joseph rests his tired head on the bed next to William.

Hours later, an almighty loud coughing breaks the early morning silence. William grips Joseph's hand as he deals with the intense pain. Wheeze after wheeze, cough after cough, Joseph tries to steady him. Then as the coughing calms, William slowly opens his bloodshot eyes. The first thing he sees is a very tired-looking Joseph, smiling at him.

"How are you feeling?" asks Joseph.

"Like a horse has trampled over me," William replies in a hoarse voice.

The more they talk, the louder the conversation grows. The chatter halts when there's a knock on the bedroom door and in walks a sleepy Rose.

"I'm sorry if we woke you," says Joseph.

"It's alright," says Rose. "I'm glad you're awake. You gave us such a fright," she adds, looking towards William. Rose's appearance reminds Joseph of their exciting news. He stands up next to her as she rubs her stomach and they look at each other tenderly, then turn their attention to William.

Joseph says, "I know this may not be the right time to share this but we're so excited." His eyes are sparkling, teeth beaming and cheeks rigidly high as if pulled by string. He stands, oozing with pride for himself and Rose as they both squeeze each other's hands, practically jumping on the spot. "We are going to have a baby!" they announce together.

"Congratulations to the two of you," says William in a raspy whisper.

"Exactly. Congratulations to us," Rose says. "So if you want to meet your grandson, you're just going to have to get better."

After a few hours of sleep, Rose and Joseph help William wash and get into clean clothes. Rose leaves the room to make breakfast, while Joseph stays with William. William starts coughing violently again. Joseph tries his best to help but feels useless. As the coughing settles down, Joseph can sense the distress in William's eyes.

"Are you alright?" asks a concerned Joseph.

"Umhum," responds William through gritted teeth.

Uncomfortable, nervous and worried, Joseph isn't

sure what to do. He sits, waiting anxiously. The coughing starts again. William's face turns red from straining intensely.

As the coughing becomes relentless, William signals Joseph with an outstretched hand and arm for the chamber bowl on the side. Handing him the pot in the nick of time, William to produces a dark red bile from his mouth.

At that moment, Rose walks in and the terrifying sight in front of her causes her to drop the tray carrying their breakfast. Joseph glances in Rose's direction, as she starts gathering everything back onto the tray with shaky hands.

"Rose, when you take that stuff back downstairs, would you go to the William's house and ask Robert to come straight here, please?" says Joseph anxiously.

As Rose leaves to fetch the doctor, Joseph continues to help William. Once the gut wrenching coughing subsides, William lays back down slowly. His hair is pointing in all directions, his face is red and swollen, and his eyes are bloodshot, half closed and roll around deliriously.

Joseph is trying his up most to keep his crushing fear at bay, desperately wanting to help and yet falling to a complete loss on what to do.

He has never felt so helpless, sitting there beside the bed, holding William's hand. It feels like Rose has been gone forever.

Suddenly, William's grip holding his hand becomes limp. Joseph glances at the two hands and William's hand has fallen to one side slightly. He looks at his face. His eyes are fully closed like he is sleeping.

Joseph's bottom lip quivers as he lifts himself off the chair to place his head on William's motionless chest.

At that moment, Joseph is briefly distracted by the sound of movement of multiple people climbing the stairs. Within seconds the door swings open and Robert rushes in to examine William's body, checking the forehead then the wrist for a pulse.

Joseph can only watch with a look of desperation across his face.

"I'm very sorry, Joseph. William has passed."

Unable to hold back any longer, Joseph lets out a stomach churning cry as he lays his head onto the lifeless body, his hand gripping the covers with knuckle-whitening force.

Robert heads out of the room, guiding Rose to do the same.

In the kitchen, she tries to make herself busy by cleaning, organising the storage and sweeping the floor.

A little while later, she ventures upstairs with a cup of tea and places it on the side. She sits next to Joseph and gently rubs his shoulders.

"I'm so sorry for your loss," she whispers solemnly.

Joseph sends a letter to his parents pleading for their presence but they reply with their apologies and condolences (saying they were unable to make it, after they had been run out of town and wouldn't feel welcome).

A whole week passes before the day of the funeral arrives. Everyone follows the horse drawn carriage to the church. It is to be a very simple affair, with the congregation a mixture of William's friends and his most loyal customers – and, of course, Joseph and Rose.

The priest commences the service and invites William's closest friends up to the lectern to express their grief and share their stories and memories.

Joseph feels numb and can't process anything. His eyes are tightly shut with only tears escaping. He rocks back and forth gently and alternates between rubbing his palms together and rubbing them heavily on his thighs. Rose sits beside him, mustering her own inner strength and holding his upper arm, trying to console him.

The priest says, "Joseph, my child, would you like to say a few words?"

Upon hearing his name, his body becomes stiff and he slowly opens his swollen bloodshot eyes. Looking at the priest, he turns to Rose and swallows. He lifts himself up to his feet with Rose's aid. With nothing written or prepared, he slowly makes his way up to the lectern.

Standing there, his eyes scan the congregation before casting them over the wooden coffin. His bottom lip quivers and he says in a shaky and weak voice, "William was my best friend. He showed me kindness. He taught me how to make and build." Unable to fight back the tears, he drops to his knees and places a hand on the coffin. Using his other hand, he wipes his reddening face,

which is streaming in tears and snot. He stutters, "G...
Goodbye F... F... Father!" A sobbing Joseph caresses
his palms against the coffin in grief, reaching for William.

Some of the congregation gasp and others look at each
other with their mouths wide open in disbelief.

Rose rushes forward and, with the help of the priest,
Joseph is helped back to his seat.

Sitting with a fist resting on each leg, anger floods
his body and his clenched hands grow tighter until his
knuckles whiten. Joseph remembers himself, takes a deep
breath and regains his composure.

The priest attempts to continue the service but is
interrupted by Joseph taking to his feet once more, wiping
his tears, brushing the dust off his knees and breathing
back the ebb of each sob. Clearing his hoarse and brittle
throat, he eyes the priest who stiffens.

"I'm sorry, father."

The priest, resigned, smiles gently to Joseph who turns
his body before the congregation.

"You all know I love him. William is my father... *was* my
father. I don't have to say anything to you all. I remember
how you treated my family. I remember your hate. You
can all keep your hate. He was too good for you, all of
you. Myself included." He returns to his seat, fidgeting
with his hands as a tear falls from each eye.

The priest continues the service, bringing it to a thoughtful
conclusion, bowing his head. Then the undertaker signals
the pallbearers and they gracefully and silently assume

their places, before, like a military manoeuvre, they respectfully lift the coffin up onto their shoulders without a flicker of emotion. The men march in step as the coffin is taken outside. Joseph looks at Rose and places his hand on her shoulder by way of suggesting they leave and they walk out down the aisle. Passing through the church entrance, his hands shake and his pulse thrums. The rest of the congregation hang back and follow the couple outside.

They all congregate and stand around a rectangular hole in the ground with a mound of soil piled to one side. The priest says the Lord's Prayer as the coffin is gradually lowered down to the bottom, then the priest casts holy water over it.

"In the name of the Father... the Son... the Holy Spirit... amen," says the priest as he makes the sign of the cross using his hands.

Joseph, along with a few others, grabs a small handful of dirt and throws it down to the coffin and mutters, "Goodbye, Father. Love you." He turns and hugs a weeping Rose. They embrace each other for support.

Once the funeral is over, Joseph and Rose delicately organise William's possessions the best they can with help from Robert and Esme. Then after learning the house and workshop were owned by the church, they decide to return to London using a similar horse drawn coach to the one they arrived in.

Upon returning to the capital, Joseph organises a wake in memory of William in the public house. Rose and her father, along with Joseph's parents and siblings reminisce over William's life.

Joseph stands and says after tapping a fork against a glass, "We remember William. A hard working man, my best friend. He took me under his wing and helped me through some difficult times." Then raising his glass to toast, Joseph states, "To William."

The whole room raise their glasses and repeat the same.

Staying on his feet, he continues. "While we were in Hopewood, I couldn't have made it through it all without my wonderful wife, Rose." He beckons her over to join him, smiling with tears in his eyes. Rose stands beside Joseph shyly, when he says, "Rose has made me the happiest man in the world and we want to share the great news. We are going to have a baby."

Joseph has no sooner made the announcement, when they are swamped by elated family members and tears of joy.

EPILOGUE

Eight months later, Rose gives birth to a handsome baby boy on September 29th 1896. One evening a few day's later, Joseph is sitting in front of the fireplace after a hard day's work. He comforts Rose as she breastfeeds the baby.

As they both admire their son, consumed by unconditional love, Rose says, "We should think of a name. It's tradition to name the first born after their father. What do you think?"

"I'm not sure," replies Joseph as he ponders.

"I'm sure we could use one of the grandfather's names," Rose suggests. Then her eyes light up and she says with a glint in her eye, "I know a great name: William. We should name him William? Yes, William Richard Joseph Adams – it's perfect."

"Yes… you are right it *is* perfect," agrees Joseph.

As they cradle their son, William, Joseph can't help but remember his time spent in the Wood and how running away never fixed any of his problems. He thought of a girl who showed kindness beyond her years and taught him how to be brave.

As Rose finishes feeding and winding the baby, Joseph is snapped back to reality by Rose asking, "Can you hold the baby for a few minutes while I go and make a cup of tea."

"Yes, no problem," answers Joseph as Rose lays their bundle of joy into his arms.

As Rose leaves the room, he looks into William's eyes and a feeling of all-consuming love spreads through his whole body. And as a tiny hand grips his finger, Joseph becomes lost in the baby's gaze and begins to talk quietly… "William Richard Joseph Adams. That's a great name, your mother is right. And you're named after a great man." Joseph looks over at his polished box with charred edges as it sits on top of the drawers in the corner of the room.

While still cradling the baby, Joseph lifts himself up, collects the box and sits back down. "This box is very special to me. It was made for me by the man you're named after," Joseph says as he balances the box on his thigh and, after carefully feeling the carved surface, opens the lid.

A flood of memories roll through his mind as his eyes survey the carved figures. He picks up the most important one and says, "Look here," as he rolls it between his fingers. "This one is meant to be the man you're named after, William. My real father. Your grandfather. It's not excellent like his carvings are or ever were. I carved it myself from memory. I made his face quite well though, I think."

Rose, carrying the cups of tea on a tray, makes her way back to the room but she stops short of the doorway to overhear Joseph talking to the baby.

"William was a great man. He taught me all about

wood and the beautiful things we can make. When you're bigger, I'll show you. He showed me kindness when most people wouldn't look at me," continues Joseph.

Rose's eyes well up and her hands begin to tremble a little. She takes a deep breath to calm herself and continues to listen.

"I remember when he would take me into the Wood for timber. He'd explain how to tell what each tree was by their leaves. I loved every minute I spent with him and that's why he made me this box and figures. I think this box should be yours now. I hope you enjoy it as much as I did," says Joseph.

Sensing he's finished, Rose then enters, sits down, places the tray on her lap and quickly wipes away a tear welling in her eye. She glances down at the box and says, "Have you shown him your figures?"

"I told him it's a special box for a special boy, so it now belongs to him," replies Joseph, before kissing the now sleeping William on the forehead.

The End.

Author's note

I appreciate you reading my book and I hope you enjoyed it. I wrote this book about acceptance and to help others have a better understanding and try to view the world through different eyes.

Extract:

He then pauses for a moment and rubs his chin with his hand, "I may be wrong but I think he has a medical condition. I've been hearing about it in some of my professional circles. Joseph definitely has a look of it. But with some help and care and a safe place to stay, I think he'll be just fine," says Robert.

This is the medical condition Dr Robert diagnoses Joseph with and I'd like to explain the meaning behind it:

Down's syndrome

A baby with Down's syndrome is born with more of chromosome 21 in some or all of the cells that make up their DNA. It's also known as Trisomy 21.

People with Down's syndrome may lead active, healthy and independent lives into their 60s, 70s and beyond. Most will have mild to moderate learning disabilities and some may have more complex needs. It cannot be known before birth if a person will need any additional help and support.
Source: www.nhsinform.scot

Thank you.

A huge thank you to the following people:

Anna,
Natalie,
Lisa,
Spencer,
Lisa.

Printed in Great Britain
by Amazon

38140960R00098